A Dead Man in
Naples

Also by Michael Pearce

A Dead Man in
Naples

MICHAEL PEARCE

Constable • London

Constable & Robinson Ltd
3 The Lanchesters
162 Fulham Palace Road
London W6 9ER
www.constablerobinson.com

First published in the UK by Constable,
an imprint of Constable & Robinson, 2009

First US edition published by SohoConstable,
an imprint of Soho Press, 2009

Soho Press, Inc.
853 Broadway
New York, NY 10003
www.sohopress.com

A copy of the British Library Cataloguing in Publication
Data is available from the British Library

UK ISBN: 978-1-84901-081-8

US ISBN: 978-1-56947-607-9
US Library of Congress number: 2009026010

Printed and bound in the EU

1 3 5 7 9 10 8 6 4 2

Mixed Sources
Product group from well-managed
forests and other controlled sources
www.fsc.org Cert no. SA-COC-1565
© 1996 Forest Stewardship Council
FSC

Chapter One

The bishop held up the round crystal box so that everyone could see. Inside were two phials of antique glass. Through the crystal you could see that each phial had a black dot inside it. Everyone – unusually in Naples – was silent. The minutes passed.

Suddenly the crowd stirred. Those nearest the box gasped. The black dot in each phial was changing, losing its darkness and becoming bright red, losing its solidity and becoming a liquid.

'Twenty-one minutes,' muttered the man standing next to Seymour. 'Twenty-one minutes. Is that what you make it?'

Seymour looked at his watch.

'Pretty well,' he agreed.

'No, no. Exactly. It's got to be exact. Twenty-one minutes. Would you say that?'

'Well, yes –'

The man darted away.

'He's gone to place a bet,' whispered Richards.

'A bet?'

'Yes. In the lottery. He's using the time the blood takes to liquefy. Twenty-one minutes. That's the number he'll use. He thinks it God-given, you see. God determines the moment when the blood turns. It's a special moment and so a special number. Maybe it will work for him, too. Of course, others will be thinking the same thing so he's got to get there first.'

1

'Not a chance,' said a man in the crowd dismissively. 'They've got a system of signals, you see. A man at the front gets the exact moment and then he signals that to someone else at the back of the crowd and he sets off at the run.'

'They take it that seriously?' said Seymour, amazed.

'Oh, yes. It's a matter of life or death, you could say.'

The crowd of assembled dignitaries and assorted rabble began to break up.

'That system's no good,' said a man standing nearby. 'Everyone uses it these days. Me, I'm going for something different this year.'

'Oh, yes?' said his neighbour. 'What's that?

'Number 13. That's the number the Englishman was wearing when he was stabbed. No one else will have thought of that.'

When Seymour had been told that he was to go to Naples, he had gone along to the Foreign Office to glean what details he could of the murdered diplomat.

The man at the Foreign Office had pursed his lips.

'Scampion,' he had said, rather reluctantly, 'was not, I am afraid, altogether satisfactory. As a consular representative that is. In himself he was a lovely man – went to Haileybury. But as a senior official in an important consulate . . .' He shook his head. 'Enthusiastic, of course. Very. In fact –' he shook his head again, this time more definitely – 'that was part of the problem.'

'Enthusiasm?'

'Yes.'

'And . . . what form exactly did it take?'

'Bicycling.'

'Bicycling!'

'Always at the edge of the new, that's where he felt he ought to be. I don't hold with it myself. If God had meant us to bicycle, he would have given us wheels, not legs. Oh, I know that in the Foreign Office we should keep abreast of the latest technology, but – what's wrong with the traditional carriage, I'd like to know? I prefer a landau, myself. But Scampion, well, as soon as he got to Italy he took up bicycling. Of course, it was all the rage. Especially among the young men.' He looked at Seymour significantly. 'The Sursum Corda, for instance.'

Sursum Corda? Wasn't that something to do with religion? He was losing the thread.

'There has always been, of course, a strong link between the Church and the army. Especially in Italy. The club he joined consisted mostly of young army officers.'

'The Sursum Corda?'

'Exactly.' He held up his hand. 'I know what you're going to say. What is wrong with that? Fine young men, good families. Well connected. Just the sort of men we want our people to be mixing with. The trouble was that it was the Sursum Corda.'

'Religious?'

'Patriotic.'

'Well –'

He held up his hand again.

'I know what you are going to say: isn't that what you would expect them to be?'

'Well, yes.'

'But it's not what you would expect a senior member of a British consulate to be.'

'No?'

'No. Patriotism is all very well, but it's got to be on behalf of the right country; your own.'

'And Scampion . . .?'

'Was patriotic about someone else's country: Italy.'

'Italy?'

'It came to a head over the war.'

War? What war was this?

'Italy's war with Libya. It may have escaped you,' said the man from the Foreign Office kindly.

'Well –'

'It started two years ago. When all the Great Powers were carving up Africa. The British, of course, were the first. We took Egypt.'

3

'Yes, yes, I remember now.'

'The French took Morocco.'

Seymour actually knew something about this.

'Germany got involved. And Spain. Well, Italy didn't want to miss out. So it invaded Libya.'

'I see.'

'The war was very popular. In Italy, that was. Less of course, in Libya. And it was particularly popular in the army.'

'The young officers?'

'Exactly. They were especially keen. And even more so the ones in the Sursum Corda.'

'The patriotic ones?'

'Exactly. Especially when the army announced that it was forming a mounted bicycle brigade. And that was when he completely lost his head.'

'Scampion?'

'Scampion. He tried to volunteer. Of course, we weren't having that. We had to put our foot down. Our policy is strict neutrality. If the Italians lose and get taken down a peg, that suits us fine. And if they win, well, it's only Arabs, anyway. No, our policy is to keep out of it. And a very good policy, too, as we keep telling the government. If only they would listen.'

'But Scampion –'

'Wouldn't keep out of it. He became very enthusiastic about the war and went round telling everyone what a good idea it was. It was the people he was mixing with, of course. The young officers. And the journalists. There was a big bicycling press in Florence, where he was at the time, and they were immensely patriotic. Bicycling rallies all over the place. Ride for victory, that sort of thing.

'But it wasn't just the racing. Through the journalists, and through his army friends, he came in touch with a lot of very strange people. D'Annunzio, for instance. You know about D'Annunzio? No? Lucky you! A complete poseur, in my opinion, but very popular with the young. A poet! Well, I ask you. Poetry is all very well, I quite like it myself. "The Charge of the Light Brigade" and that sort of thing. But *his* poetry is totally incomprehensible. And the young lap it up! It leads them astray. Into wildnesses of all sorts.

'Well, that's D'Annunzio for you. And that was the man Scampion took up with. They went round together everywhere. Scampion was even his second.'

'His second?'

'In a duel. With a journalist. D'Annunzio lost, I am glad to say, but his opponent was so appalled at the injuries he had inflicted that he apologized. So D'Annunzio claimed he had won! And retired to the loving embraces of a Marchesa, two ballerinas, an actress, and a dubious young man who works in a hotel.'

'And Scampion?'

'Was mixed up in this lot,' said the diplomat with disgust. 'It became so bad that we had to transfer him to Naples. Where, of course, he formed a Racing Club and carried on much as he had done before.'

'With the officers?'

'Different ones. There's a big camp outside Naples. A transit camp. For soldiers on their way to Libya. He organized bicycle races every Saturday. And it was claimed at the inquest that it was rivalry arising out of one of these races that led to him being stabbed.'

Seymour considered.

When the Chief Superintendent had told him that he could expect to be sent to Naples, his heart had leaped. Would not that be the answer to his difficulties?

Chief among these difficulties was his girlfriend, Chantale, whom he had at last persuaded to leave her native Mediterranean and build a life with him in sunny London. Actually, he had been honest about that. She would find, he had told her, that the skies in London were not quite as blue as those in Tangier, her home town, the sun not quite as hot, the water of the East London docks not quite as sparkling.

It had turned out to be all that, said Chantale; but worse.

She had taken lately to scanning the travel pages of the newspapers, which offered holidays in Tenerife, Luxor,

5

Madeira, and the Maldives. No chance, said Seymour. The best he could offer on his pay was a day trip to Brighton, which was not, in her view, quite the same thing.

So the prospect of Naples had come as a gift from heaven. Chantale could surely be smuggled somehow into his baggage and two could occupy a room, or a bed, as cheaply as one.

Now, however, as he was speaking to the man from the Foreign Office, honesty, a rare and not always a helpful quality in a policeman, compelled him to say:

'Look, this is all very interesting, but I don't quite see why it should have been necessary to send for me. Surely the local police –'

'One would think so,' said the man from the Foreign Office glumly, 'and that we could have happily forgotten all about Scampion. Unfortunately it is not quite so simple.'

'No?'

'To start with, the claim that he was stabbed because of rivalries arising out of his racing was not sustained at the inquest. The verdict was left open. The claim was quite preposterous anyway. Not that that mattered too much: at least it meant that the whole business would be shelved for a while and then, perhaps, could conveniently be forgotten about.

'But then we received a tip. From a quite discreditable source, of course: the Roman aristocracy. Discreditable, but well-informed, especially about what is going on in ministerial circles. So we could not afford to ignore it. It was to the effect that Scampion's death was connected with politics at the highest level and that he had been on the edge of revealing something that would cause an enormous breach in international relations. And that the newspapers had got hold of this and would very shortly be in a position to publish what they knew.

'We will deny it, of course. Whatever it is. But it would be helpful if we knew in advance exactly *what* it is that we would be denying. That, Mr Seymour, is where you come in. What exactly had Scampion been up to? What was the secret he had allegedly found out, the real reason for his murder? Oh, and, of course, although this is not terribly important, who actually killed him?'

His investigation was, said the man at the Foreign Office, to be 'unofficial'. Seymour knew what that meant. It meant that, if anything went wrong, he could safely be disowned. Seymour, however, after one or two of these 'unofficial' assignments, was growing wiser in the ways of the world and the more he thought about this, the less he liked it. If things went wrong he could see himself spending the rest of his life in some disease-ridden Neapolitan jail. He had almost decided to decline it. Since it was an 'unofficial' assignment, he could do that. He wouldn't be popular but he would get away with it. It would jeopardize his long-term career prospects but living, as opposed to dying, might be worth it.

He had, however, incautiously mentioned the matter to Chantale and she had taken a completely different view. If it was unofficial, didn't that mean that he could do what he liked? He could, for instance, take her with him. Although that had been Seymour's own first thought, he was now backing off the idea and said that he didn't think the Foreign Office definition of unofficial stretched that far.

Chantale pondered on this. Her mind was always at its most fertile when she strongly wanted to do something and some objection by Seymour stood in the way.

'Why shouldn't it?' she asked. 'Wouldn't that give – what is the word you use for this sort of thing? Cover – yes, it would give good cover. You could pretend to be taking a holiday and what would be more natural than to take me with you? No one could possibly suspect you of being on an official assignment then. You might even get them to pay for me.'

Seymour didn't think the rubric, whether official or unofficial, would stretch that far, either, but it was worth a try. To his surprise, they agreed.

'It would certainly remove any suspicion if your wife came with you,' they said.

'Um. Actually,' said Seymour, 'not wife.'

'Ah!'

'Yet,' said Seymour hastily.

'Ah, fiancée,' said the man in Accounts. 'Well, we should be able to manage that. Accommodation is cheap in Naples. Two rooms, then.'

Seymour kept his mouth shut this time and two rooms it was. Chantale was as pleased as Punch.

Seymour, reflecting still further, saw yet another advantage in the arrangement. While if he was on his own, and something went wrong, he might safely be disowned and allowed to rot away for the rest of his days in a Neapolitan prison cell, they would find it more difficult to do that if Chantale was in the cell with him. But he didn't mention this to her.

Second – financial – thoughts had crept in at the Foreign Office and the two rooms were not now in a hotel but in a sort of boarding house or *pensione*. The *pensione* was owned by an old man, Giuseppi, whose heart was with the revolution but whose revolutionary activities these days were confined to making fierce noises, mostly about the government. It was run, however, by his wife, Maria.

As Richards was taking him through the tiny streets they went past the front of the *pensione*. Giuseppi and Maria were standing outside gazing along the street in astonishment. As was usual in Naples most front doors in the street were open and quite a few of the inhabitants had come out to gaze, too. At the end of the street was a solitary English lady holding a bicycle. That in itself would account for the astonishment but there was another cause of wonder, too.

'Indecent, I call it,' said old Giuseppi. 'Indecent, and quite mad.'

'But very practical,' said his granddaughter, Francesca, who was standing with them.

'Maybe,' said Maria, 'but don't let me ever catch *you* wearing anything like that!'

'Bicycles cost money,' said Francesca. 'Would you ever see me on one?'

'Yes,' said her grandfather. 'I saw you on one yesterday.'

'Francesca!' said his wife.

'With young Giorgio,' said Giuseppi. 'You were sitting on the cross-bar. Showing your ankles.'

'Francesca!'

'That's the point,' said Francesca.

'What!' cried Maria. 'To show your ankles?'

'That's the point of what she's wearing. So that she should *not* show her ankles.'

'Well, don't let me ever see you wearing anything so indecent,' said her grandmother.

'They call them bloomers,' said Francesca.

'American decadence!' sneered old Giuseppi.

'There's a point to them,' insisted Francesca. 'If you're riding a bicycle.'

'Yes, but should you *be* riding a bicycle in the first place? If you're a woman?'

'Miss Scampion rides a bicycle.'

'Yes, but she's English and probably doesn't know any better.'

'And she's rich,' said Giuseppi. 'If you're rich, you can get away with anything.'

'Don't ever –' began Maria.

'It's fashionable,' cried Francesca. '*Fashionable*!'

'Listen,' said old Giuseppi, 'it wasn't fashion that young Giorgio was interested in when you were sitting on his bicycle showing him your ankles!'

'For God's sake!' cried Francesca, and ran off indoors.

Seymour and Richards walked on up the street. The English lady, still holding her bicycle uncertainly, broke into a smile when she saw them arriving.

'Mr Richards!' she said with relief.

'Miss Scampion! Can I be of any assistance?'

'I'm afraid I've rather lost my way.'

'Where are you making for?'

'The Porta Capuana.'

'Ah, well, you've strayed somewhat from your path, then. But we'll soon put you back on it.' He looked at the bicycle. 'I think, perhaps, you'd better walk. The streets are very narrow here.'

'May I?' said Seymour, putting his hand on the bicycle. 'Thank you.'

'This is Mr Seymour,' said Richards. 'He's visiting us.'

'How do you do, Mr Seymour. Are you in Naples for long?'

'A few weeks, I anticipate.'

'Seymour is on holiday. With his fiancée.'

'Oh, how nice! A sort of anticipatory honeymoon?'

'Sort of.'

Miss Scampion laughed. 'Well, I hope it goes very nicely for you.'

'Back at home Seymour is a policeman,' said Richards.

Miss Scampion looked at him sharply. 'Really?'

'He's from Scotland Yard.'

'And – and he's here on *holiday*?'

'He might look at some other things in passing.'

'And the fiancée?'

'Mostly I shall be looking at her,' said Seymour.

'She's a real fiancée, then?'

'Genuine flesh and blood,' said Richards. 'I've seen her.'

'And is she pretty?'

'Astonishingly so.'

'I expect you concur, Mr Seymour.'

'I do, indeed.'

'And you are going to marry her?'

'If she doesn't change her mind.'

'You are a fortunate man, Mr Seymour.' She sighed. 'Unlike my brother. He never had much luck with women.'

'Oh, I don't know,' objected Richards. 'Whenever I saw him, he seemed to be doing pretty well.'

'Ah, but not in my sense. And not, I think, in Mr Seymour's sense. Lionel certainly always had a lot of striking women around him when we were in Florence but I

10

think that was a matter less of his own skill than of the skills of others.'

'What exactly do you mean by that, Miss Scampion?' asked Seymour.

She smiled. 'It was the crowd he hung out with. And I don't think they did him much good. In the end.'

He would have liked to have asked her more but then she stopped.

'I think I know where I am now. The Porta del Carmine is just over there, is it not? Is the Porta del Carmine where you are taking Mr Seymour?'

'Well —'

'I will come with you,' said Miss Scampion firmly.

'Are you sure? Will it not . . .?'

'Prove distressing? Yes. But I would like to see what Mr Seymour makes of it.'

'The Porta del Carmine was where, sadly . . .'

'My brother was murdered,' said Miss Scampion unflinchingly, and led on with her bicycle.

The Porta del Carmine was marked by two strange-looking columns. They were not smooth pillars carved from a simple piece of stone but seemed to have been constructed by piling great, square slabs of stone on top of each other. The slabs in the right-hand column had a reddish tinge, those in the left-hand one a yellowish tinge. Both columns were crowned by further slabs arranged to form a queer kind of hat.

'Here,' said Miss Scampion, stopping at the base of the left-hand column. 'This is where it happened. He had just dismounted from his bicycle because he did not wish to ride through the piazza.'

'He was on a bicycle, then?'

'He was just on his way home after racing. He was a very keen road-racer, Mr Seymour. He went out on his bicycle most evenings and raced with his club on Saturdays. Which was what he had been doing that morning.'

Seymour could understand why Scampion had not attempted to ride through the piazza. Every inch of it was covered. There were carts, barrows and great ox-wagons.

There were caravans of mules and herds of goats. Donkeys stood patiently by the stalls and chickens ran around under the feet of the passers-by. The stalls were loaded with fruit – melons, oranges and grapes glowing in the sun – and vegetables: onions as big as children's heads, tomatoes as big as footballs, aubergines bursting with ripeness, peas, beans and lettuces, cucumbers as big as clubs, chestnuts in great long strings. There were cuts of meat, sausages, black puddings, together with biscuits, cakes and sweets, as well as the usual assortment of haberdashery, knick-knacks and holy images and rosaries.

And, of course, milling in and out of the carts and animals and clustering round the stalls were hundreds, if not thousands, of people talking – well, not talking, shouting – gesticulating, bargaining, gossiping. The square was huge, huge enough to lose any normal amount of noise. Here it hadn't a chance.

Seymour went over to where Miss Scampion was standing.

'Right here?' he said.

'Right here.'

'Someone stepped out from behind the column,' said Richards, 'and stabbed him.'

'Just like that?'

'Just like that. Apparently.'

'Did anyone see it?'

'No. That is not unusual in Naples.'

'Was anything taken? His wallet, for instance?'

'He wasn't carrying one. He never did when he was racing. He didn't want to be carrying anything that wasn't strictly necessary. He said it reduced his speed. He carried a few small coins and a single note, in case of emergency.'

'The coins were found afterwards beside his body,' said Miss Scampion.

'That, too, is unusual in Naples,' said Richards drily.

'They appear to have come out as he fell.'

'And the note?'

'Was still in his pocket.'

'So it wasn't money, then?'

12

'No.'

'But what else could it have been?' cried Miss Scampion passionately. 'Lionel didn't have an enemy in the world. He was the most inoffensive of men.'

'Wouldn't harm a soul,' Richards concurred.

'Try as I might, Mr Seymour, I cannot think of any reason why anyone would want to kill him.'

'Of course, we can never know all –' began Richards.

Miss Scampion cut him short. 'But in this case, Mr Richards, I do know all! He was my brother, Mr Seymour. We have lived together all our lives, or at least since Oxford. We were very close. He had no secrets from me nor I from him. If there was something in any of his relationships to make him uneasy, I would have known. Anything which might lead someone to want to kill him. But there was nothing. Nothing! I am absolutely sure of it.'

'Of course,' said Richards, 'there may have *been* no reason.'

'I am afraid I do not understand you, Mr Richards.'

'No *particular* reason, that is.'

'One does not step out from behind a column and stab someone for no reason at all, Mr Richards!'

'Well, one might.'

'If one were mad, you mean?' Miss Scampion shuddered. 'That is a terrible thought! But possible, I suppose.'

'Or if one had some sort of enmity towards foreigners. Naples is an inward-looking city, Miss Scampion, and does not always welcome strangers. It might have been enough that your brother was obviously a foreigner.'

'That, too, is a terrible thought,' said Miss Scampion.

'And possibly completely without foundation,' said Richards hastily. 'I mention it only to suggest that there may have been nothing in your brother's life to bring on this terrible attack.'

'But if it is as pointless as you suggest, that somehow makes it even worse,' said Miss Scampion. 'It seems as bad as what appears to be the popular supposition, or so our cleaner tells me, that it was something to do with the Camorra.'

'That is always the general supposition when something untoward happens in Naples,' said Richards. 'That the Camorra has something to do with it. But, believe me, Miss Scampion, even the Camorra does not kill without reason.'

'The Camorra?' asked Seymour.

'A secret society. *The* secret society in Naples. The Mafia in Sicily, the Camorra in Naples. A distasteful institution, certainly, but rational in its way. It does not kill without reason.'

'And what reason could there be so far as Lionel was concerned? He had never had anything to do with the Camorra. That I can swear!'

'Nor any of us, Miss Scampion. In the consulate we steer clear of the Camorra.'

'But then,' said Miss Scampion, beginning to tremble, 'who *would* have wanted to kill such a good, good man?'

'Miss Scampion,' said Seymour, 'I feel you may be disturbing yourself – *we* may be disturbing you – unnecessarily.'

'Yes, yes, of course!' said Richards hurriedly. 'So I am afraid we are. This must be all very painful for you. May I suggest that you continue on to the Porta Capuana? I will escort you there.'

'Perhaps it would be best,' said Miss Scampion reluctantly. 'I do not wish to distract Mr Seymour.' She smiled bravely. 'There is nothing worse than an interfering woman. That is what my brother used to say when he was cross with me.'

She began to move away.

But then she looked back over her shoulder.

'However, I *am* going to interfere, Mr Seymour. Or, if not interfere, be a nuisance. I am going to stay in Naples until I have found out who murdered my brother. I know your superiors are fed up with me, Mr Richards – I know that they would prefer me to go back to England. But I will not. Not until I have found out who killed my brother. And made them pay for it.'

* * *

14

When Richards was gone, Seymour explored the area around the great Gate. While in front of it stretched the huge open piazza, behind it was a warren of tiny streets. In one of them, just along from the Porta, was a snail shop. It consisted of a large copper cauldron over a charcoal stove right in the middle of the street, almost blocking the way. Around it several men were sitting. Mostly they sat on the ground, which didn't help passage at all; but there was also a rickety table with two cane chairs. At the table a man was sitting reading a book. He looked up at Seymour and politely indicated the chair opposite him. Seymour sat down and the proprietor put a bowl in front of him and poured some of the contents of the cauldron into it.

'They are really quite good,' said the man opposite him. 'I live just along the street – I am a carpenter, I have a shop there – and come every day for my lunch. It is a change from the shop, and also a relief for my wife. Or so she says.'

Seymour laughed.

'Don't let me interrupt your reading,' he said.

'Oh, I'm just checking my bets,' said the man.

'Checking . . .?'

'It's a Smorfia.'

Seeing that Seymour did not understand, he showed it him. It appeared to be a kind of lottery dictionary which gave a numeric value to almost any event which could happen in the city.

'People use it,' said the man, 'to decide on a number to play in the lottery. For example, suppose you saw a woman run over by a cab. You might think that was a lucky sign and want to use it. The problem would be to find a number for it. That's where the Smorfia helps you. Look, I'll show you.'

He opened the Smorfia.

'Woman, that's 22. Cab, either 41 or 78, depending on whether the cab was empty or had passengers. Street, well, that would, of course, depend on where it was, but let's say 53. Accident is 17. So now you've got the numbers: 22, 78, 53 and 17.

'Now you have to decide how to play them. For example, if you decide to play on two numbers – that's an *ambo* – you might pick 22 and 17. But you could go for a *terno* and play three numbers.'

'Suppose,' said Seymour, 'I went for a murder. A man, say. Here, at the Porta Carmine.'

'That would be 15, 13 and 27. Are you going to play it?'

'I might,' said Seymour.

The man looked at his watch. 'They'll be drawing the next numbers in about ten minutes. Why don't you go along?'

The drawing of the numbers was done in public so that everyone could see there was no fraud about it. It started with officials coming out of the Exchequer and sitting in a row on a balcony overlooking the courtyard. Ninety paper labels with numbers on them were shown in succession and each one was put in a brass ball, the two halves of which were then screwed together and thrown into a huge glass box shaped like a wheel which revolved at the touch of a handle.

A child dressed in white came forward and drew out one of the balls. It was unscrewed and the number taken out, displayed and proclaimed. Then the handle was worked again and another ball taken out.

'Well,' said the carpenter, peering eagerly, 'did your numbers come up?'

Seymour looked at his tickets.

'No,' he said, 'not this time.'

Chapter Two

Seymour divided the contents of Scampion's desk into three piles. The first pile was consular business. Most of it appeared to be to do with Visitors – important ones, judging by the capital letter in the file. It consisted largely of itineraries he had drawn up for them. Attached to the itineraries were often private notes to himself.

'Professor Caldicott. Classicist. Wants to see Paestum. *Not* Pompeii Again! Try Baiae.'

'Mrs Faith Widdorson. Wants to see churches. Angevin ones the first day, Aragonese the second?'

To which was added a later pencilled note: 'Complains all Catholic! What the hell does she expect in Italy? Note: is there a Plymouth Brethren church in Naples?'

'The Wainwrights. North country. Manufacturing, I suspect. Stinking rich. Want to see "the sights". Nightclubs?'

A later note: 'No. At least, not her, him, perhaps, probably without wife knowing. She, "Something romantic." Bay of Naples at sunset?'

Yet a later note: 'How much would it cost to buy the Bay of Naples?!'

And: 'Miss Daphne Dillacourt. Unattached female of certain age. Watch it! Suggest Capri.'

Added note in pencil: 'Don't go with her next time.'

Another note, later: 'Wants Capri again. *Don't* go with her!'

And a third, slightly desperate: 'Capri *again*! *Don't* go with her. And make it a slow boat.'

Yet a fourth: 'Make it even slower. And *find someone else!* Antonio?'

There was a lady whose name featured several times.

'Who is this "Sybil"?' he asked Richards.

Richards peered over his shoulder. 'I take it you're not a classicist, old man?'

'Well, no . . .'

'*The* Sybil. Of Cumae. Legendary figure mentioned in Virgil. Had gift of foretelling the future.'

'Oh!'

'Every man in Naples has been looking for her ever since. To help him place his bets.'

'Not around now, I take it?'

'No. But Cumae is. By Avernus, the legendary entrance to Hell. Go there and you'll believe it.'

'Hmm.'

Richards sat back. 'Actually, I'm not a classicist, either. Commerce is more my line. And that, as a matter of fact, is more useful in most consulates. Even in Naples.'

Seymour glanced again at the first file.

'That's funny,' he said. 'I haven't found much apart from visitors.'

'You wouldn't. Kept him away from the real work. Too important to let him cock it up.'

'Like that, was it?'

'Yes. If you were charitable, you could say his gifts were more for the social. In fact, too much for the social. That's why they sent him down here. To get him away from the crowd he was with in Florence.'

'So they posted him to Naples? Well, that was no hardship, was it?'

'Not for him,' said Richards.

Seymour looked at him.

'But it was for me,' said Richards. 'I had to do his work. They told me I would be posted away. We're on the same grade, you see, and there wasn't room for the two of us. But then the stupid bastard got himself killed!'

'And you had to stay on? Well, I don't expect you minded that, did you?'

'Actually, I did. It doesn't do in the consular service to get stuck in a post and I wanted to move on.'

The second pile was larger and consisted entirely of matters to do with bicycling. Here, too, there were itineraries in plenty. They took the form now, though, of notes for road races. Routes were listed, starting places and finishes. Again there were the added notes.

'Long stretch uphill between Valdosa and Berindi. Will sort out the sheep from the goats!'

'Hairpin. Don't go into it too fast. Steep drop on one side. *Warn people!*'

'Paisi. Road suddenly narrows. Will race have thinned out by that time? We don't want too many people going into that bit together.'

There were more names here, mostly, judging by the fact that sometimes ranks were given, army officers. They were often in connection with race-marshalling, officials to oversee the start and finish of the race, a few posted around to help at significant spots. With one man in particular there was a lot of correspondence. He was referred to only by his Christian name, Vincente, who seemed to be Scampion's racing alter ego at the nearby army base.

'A lot here to do with racing and bicycles,' Seymour said to Richards.

'At least it got him out of the way,' said Richards.

The third pile was completely different. It consisted entirely of private letters, all from the same person, a woman. Most of them were on headed – indeed, crested – notepaper. The sender appeared to be a Marchesa. That was not how she signed her letters, though. She signed them simply 'Luisa'.

Some were from Florence, a few from Rome. The recent ones were from Bessandro, which was the nearby army base. The most recent letter said:

So, my dear, at last I am here. What a hell-hole! I shall escape to Naples at every opportunity. Vincente feels the same but at least he has his bicycle. No such respite for me! Thank God you, at least, are here. I miss the old crowd. Gabrieli has been obliged to fly to France. For 'sexual misdemeanours'! How can a man be exiled for sexual misdemeanours? It is ridiculous. I said so to Alessandro but he doesn't take that view. He says there is a point beyond which one should not go, especially if one is active in politics, where they are always looking for an excuse to do one down. Of course, he would take that view, being himself a politician. At least no one is ever likely to accuse *him* of sexual misdemeanours. But that is not enough: Caesar's wife, too, should be above suspicion, which I am definitely not!

And so, my dear, I, too, am sent into exile and told not to come back until I am spotless. This, I am afraid, could take some time. I have complained to Vincente but he is unsympathetic. Of course, he has his bicycling. And he still hopes to be sent to Libya. Listen, I told him, I am definitely not going there!

'At least, for the moment, he is here, and so are you. You must take care, both of you, not to come to grief on these mountainous roads. My heart rises into my mouth every time I think of you both hurtling round these frightening bends. Do take care, my dear. I hope to see you soon.

Yours, as ever affectionately,
Luisa.

While Seymour was at the consulate checking through Scampion's desk a message came from Miss Scampion asking for Chantale's name and the name of their hotel as she would like to invite her to tea. And perhaps he himself would join them?

'Good heavens!' said Miss Scampion when she saw Chantale. 'She's . . .'

'Moroccan,' said Seymour.

'Yes, yes,' said Miss Scampion, recovering. 'Of course, Moroccan.' Then, still slightly flustered: 'I thought from the name that . . .'

'De Lissac,' said Seymour. 'It's a French name. Her father was French.'

'Oh, how interesting!' said Miss Scampion bravely. 'French, is it?'

'My father was stationed in Morocco,' said Chantale.

'An army officer? Well, that's good. Very good. And . . . French.'

Seymour had never really thought of Chantale as dark. She was dark, of course, in the way that Arabs and many southern Europeans are dark. Her eyes were brown and she had black hair and her skin was brownish. In the East End of London, where Seymour lived and worked, and where so many of the inhabitants were immigrants and Italians were at every street corner, she did not stand out at all. But Miss Scampion had at once made the identification.

'De Lissac,' she said now, stressing the 'de'. 'And does that mean that your father was a . . . of a good family?'

'They think so,' said Chantale shortly.

In fact, her father had never got on with his family and had broken from them when he had married Chantale's mother.

'A military family, I expect,' said Miss Scampion with approval.

'Yes.'

'It runs in families,' said Miss Scampion. 'English ones, too. We have soldiers in our family, but mostly on a different branch. My brother always regretted that he had not been a soldier. Indeed, he wanted to be attached to the Italian army when he heard they were going to Libya. But our Foreign Office was furious. I don't know why. After all, in India, which was where my relatives served, there was considerable movement between the army and the civil administration.'

She led them through the house to a small patio where a table was laid for an English tea.

'How delightful!' said Chantale.

'One does try to maintain standards,' said Miss Scampion, 'no matter where one is. That was what my uncle, my army uncle, always used to say. One mustn't let things slip. Of course, that was very important in India. You had to keep up to the mark and see that other people kept up to the mark. It was like that when he came back to England, too. As children, we found him very severe. He would fly into a rage over the smallest thing. If the cucumber were not quite crisp, for example. "It's the servants," he would say. "They don't know their job. Now, in India . . ."

'We used to laugh at him, of course, but I really think he would have been happier in India. He had been out there for so long. But then, as I'm sure you found, Miss de Lissac, life in a military garrison has such a special flavour.'

Chantale had not, in fact, spent any time in a military garrison. She had been brought up by her mother among the souks and bazaars and mosques of Tangier, which was very different. But she thought it best not to say this. It was evidently easier for Miss Scampion to come to terms with the unpalatable fact of Chantale's colour by dwelling on the other side of her origins, the army side, with which she seemed more at home and for which she seemed to have particular esteem.

Chantale, primed by Seymour, exclaimed on the niceness of the house and asked if she could be shown round it.

'Small, of course,' said Miss Scampion. 'But, then, consular salaries are small. And while in a place like Florence you get an allowance, here, in Naples, for some reason you don't.'

'It has charm,' said Chantale, 'and that is important.'

'I think so, too, my dear,' said Miss Scampion.

Over the tea table, and once she had recovered from the shock, her manner towards Chantale had thawed and she was now calling her 'my dear'. 'Delightfully young,' she whispered at one point to Seymour. 'And a good family,' said Seymour, who had never previously been known to offer any observation at all on Chantale's family; at least, not on the distant military part of it. 'It shows,' said Miss Scampion approvingly.

'And this is my brother's room,' she said.

'May I go in?' said Seymour.

Scampion had allowed his sister the better of the two bedrooms. Hers looked out over a small garden with orange trees, his merely on to the opposite side of the street. The walls were covered with pictures of bicycles and bicyclists. Some of them were group photographs which included Scampion himself. Seymour studied them carefully.

'Of course you did not know Lionel,' said Miss Scampion. 'You cannot really tell what he looked like from these – all helmets and goggles. This one gives you a better impression of him as a person.'

A round, pleasant, innocuous face. Thinning hair. A little plump despite what must be a lot of exercise. Hard to judge his height. In some of the other photographs he looked quite small. In this one, with his arm around the other man, he seemed quite big.

'That is, of course, Gabrieli,' said Miss Scampion. 'Gabrieli D'Annunzio.'

She said it as if Seymour would at once know him.

'D'Annunzio, of course,' said Seymour.

'A good man!' said Miss Scampion with emphasis. 'No matter what they say. Oh, he had his faults, I won't deny that. And there have been peccadilloes. But is there any great man without faults?'

'Miss Scampion,' said Seymour, 'would you mind if I glanced inside his desk? In the interests of – you know, the police may have missed something.'

'Very likely,' said Miss Scampion. 'No, please go ahead. I am sure he would have had no secrets to hide.'

Good heavens, yet *more* stuff to do with cycling! Brochures, catalogues, road maps, bicycling magazines. Two of them were in French, *Le Vélo* and *L'Auto-Vélo*. There were dozens of numbers of each. Miss Scampion opened one and showed an article to Seymour, pointing to the name of its author.

'He only did the one,' she said proudly. 'I urged him to do more. I felt he had a knack for it. And it might have opened up a door to another profession for him. You know, if he had been obliged to leave the service over that silly business about the war.'

'Certainly there seems to be talent there,' agreed Seymour, but I wouldn't give up the day job, he thought.

'Gabriel thought so, too. At least, I think he did. "I'd stick to prose if I were you," he said, when Lionel showed it him. Meaning, I think, that he should not go in for poetry. Well, of course, Gabriel would know about that, being such a great poet himself.'

'And you like his poetry yourself?' asked Chantale, 'D'Annunzio's, I mean?'

'Well, I can see it has great feeling,' said Miss Scampion, slightly flustered. 'But I have never entirely under-stood . . . The poetry is in the ideas, that's what my brother used to say. But I didn't quite understand that, either. Of course, the ideas are tremendous, sweeping – inspired, you may say.'

Apart from the magazines, which spilled over from the desk to some nearby shelves, there wasn't a lot in Scampion's desk. A few letters from the family at home, correspondence with the Foreign Office relating to his pay, papers connected with the renting of the house, that was about all. Seymour tried the bank statements. Often when a man is murdered there is some reflection of it in his bank balance, but there appeared to be none in Scampion's case. There wasn't much money, but there weren't many debts, either. Scampion seemed to have looked after his financial affairs with the same precise attention that he had given to organizing road races.

A few personal letters, mostly from school friends; but nothing very intimate. There weren't any further letters from the Marchesa. Was that accidental? Seymour won-dered. Or did Scampion keep that side of his life separate from his sister? Or – another thought – had his sister, guardian of her brother's flame, destroyed all the evidence of that side of his life after his death? Not, now that it

24

was in her power to do so, admitting any other rivals for his affection?

There was nothing that related to Scampion's private, emotional life. Yet this was odd, seeing that the impression Seymour had gleaned of Scampion's years in Florence had been that he was in the thick of things. What was it that Richards had said? That Scampion had been too much in the social whirl: a whirl that, again from the hints he had picked up, not least from the Marchesa, seemed to have had some nasty eddies in it.

'You are puzzled, Mr Seymour,' said Miss Scampion.

'Not really. Or, at least, yes, I am, a little. I had expected to learn more about his relationships. Your brother clearly had many friends, Miss Scampion. Certainly when he was in Florence. Yet I find no trace of them. What happened to them when he came down here?'

'He lost contact with them.'

'All of them? Isn't that a little surprising? I had the impression that in Florence he was very much in the thick of things.'

'Oh, he was! He was.'

'And yet . . .?'

'As I say, he lost them when he came down here.' She hesitated. 'They were not, perhaps, deep friends, Mr Seymour. Friends of the moment, rather. And when Gabriel moved away, they all moved with him.'

'Leaving your brother very much alone?'

'Well, of course, he had his bicycling friends. And, in any case, it was just at that moment that they decided to move him.'

'He must have felt very bereft.'

'Oh, he did. For a time he was quite at a loss. I was really rather worried about him. But then he threw himself into bicycling again and suddenly it all seemed to come right once more. But there had been moments when I feared . . .'

'Feared what, Miss Scampion?'

'That he might be going to the Bad.'

'The Bad?'

'Yes.'

'In what way, Miss Scampion?

'I couldn't put my finger on it. But I knew something was amiss. We had never had secrets from each other. But now I felt he was holding something back. And – and he *was* holding something back, Mr Seymour: this.'

She produced a little slip of paper.

'What is this?'

'A lottery ticket!' she whispered. 'I found it in his shorts this morning, the shorts he had been wearing when he was . . . They returned them to me afterwards. I had them cleaned and then put them away in a drawer. I couldn't bear to look at them. I just put them away. But then this morning I decided I must do something about them, about all his clothes. I couldn't just leave them for ever. Sooner or later I knew I would have to do something about them. So this morning I decided to face it. And I found – I found *this!*'

'In his pocket? The pocket of the shorts he had been wearing when . . .'

'Yes! It came as a shock, a great shock. Our family has always disapproved of gambling, Mr Seymour, and now to find – we have never had secrets from each other, Lionel and I, and now to find . . . to find that all the time he was . . .'

'Well, it may not have been all the time, Miss Scampion. This may have been a solitary occasion.'

'But to do it at all!' she cried. 'There was such a strong prohibition against gambling, not just in the family, but in our kirk. I couldn't believe it. That my own brother . . .'

'It may not be as you suppose, Miss Scampion. There may be a quite innocent explanation for this.'

'I know, I know! That is what I have told myself. And one shouldn't think ill of the dead. But, all the same, there it was, Mr Seymour. One must face facts. That is what my uncle used to say. And there it definitely was!'

'In his bicycling shorts? The ones he had been wearing?

'Yes. I had been going through his clothes. I thought that I must not just leave them there, I ought to put them to some *use*. I thought I might pass them on to the Church. They would know what to do with them, wouldn't they? They must know of lots of deserving cases. Lionel had a friend who was a priest, a very nice man who knew about bicycles, a Father Pepe, Pepito, they call him. I thought I would speak to him.'

'An excellent idea, Miss Scampion. And you're right, it's a task that should not be put off, however distressing. You have finished going through the clothes, have you? And found nothing further –'

'Nothing! Nothing! It was such a shock. I had to sit down.'

'I'm sure it was, Miss Scampion. Very distressing for you. But, as I say, you should not necessarily believe the worst.'

Seymour picked up the slip. It was for the City Lottery. He couldn't make out the date, the numbers had been smudged, probably in the washing, but it looked quite recent.

'Do you mind if I take this, Miss Scampion?'

He took the ticket round to the lottery office.

'You're a bit late, aren't you?'

'Well, am I? I can't make out the date.'

'It's for over a month ago. We're on a different run now.'

'Could you tell me exactly what was the date it had to be presented by?'

'Probably.'

The man took the ticket and examined it.

'It's certainly for last month and I would say it was for the eleventh. If you want, I can get it checked, but I doubt if it would be worth it. One's eyes get pretty used to this sort of thing here. You wouldn't believe how many people try to pull a fast one. Usually by altering one of the numbers. Not that I'm accusing you of anything,' he added hastily.

'I'm inquiring on behalf of a friend. Her husband died and she found this in a pocket and wondered if it was worth anything?'

The official shook his head. 'No such luck, I'm afraid. It never is, in my experience.'

The eleventh of the previous month was the day on which Scampion had died. The ticket had been one of the few things in his pockets when he had been stabbed. Could he have been on his way to present it? Seymour wondered.

Seymour was on his way back to the *pensione* when some cyclists passed him. They were not ordinary people on bicycles, but serious cyclists. They wore sporting kit, red shirts and socks, and were on what looked to Seymour like racing bicycles.

'No, no, no,' said Giuseppi. 'They're roadsters, not the ones you ride in races. This isn't the Racing Club, it's the Reds.'

'Reds?'

'Real Reds. Socialists, I mean. From Rome. They ride down to Naples occasionally to spread the word.'

'They'd do better to stay at home,' said his wife, who had come out into the street, too. 'And so would you,' she said severely, turning to her granddaughter.

'I've only come out for a minute!' protested Francesca. 'I wanted to see the cyclists.'

'At least she's come out to see some real ones,' said Giuseppi, 'not those fancy poofters.'

'They're not as good,' said Francesca critically.

'Not as good?' said Giuseppi, annoyed. 'What do you mean?'

'They don't ride as well.'

'What the hell do you know about it?'

'They're not racers,' said Francesca. 'And the thing about racing is that skills are tested out at speed. That's when you really find out if you've got them. It takes more skill to ride down a mountain fast than to do it slowly. You've got to show more control. Or else you'll come off.'

'Well, that's daft, then, isn't it? Riding more quickly than is sense.'

'Too quickly to see the beautiful world that God has provided,' said Maria.

'For heaven's sake –' began Francesca.

'Watch your tongue, my girl!'

'That's not the point of it.'

'What *is* the point, then?' demanded Giuseppi. 'The Reds have a point when they ride down from Rome. They want to tell people about socialism. They want to rouse the workers. I can see plenty of point in that. But your racers –'

'They've got a point, too. It's just a different point.'

'What is it, then?'

'They're doing it,' said Francesca loftily, 'for the sake of the challenge. For the thrills of the competition.'

'Competition! Ah, now we're getting to it. They're training to be capitalists.'

'A bicycle is not a factor of production.'

'What?' said Giuseppi, taken aback.

'According to Marx,' said Francesca. She wasn't too sure about this, actually, but saw it as a possible telling blow.

Giuseppi was, for the moment, nonplussed.

'*And* their kit is better,'said Francesca, pressing home her advantage.

'What's wrong with red shirts?' demanded Giuseppi.

'They're so out of date.'

'Out of date?'

'In the eyes of today's youth.'

'In the eyes of –? Have you been reading the newspapers again? Look, when Garibaldi marched his men through Italy to free Italy – a free Italy, does that mean nothing to you? – free Italy, from the grip of the aristocrats, the Church, –'

'Now, Giuseppi!' said Maria warningly.

'– the capitalists, and reactionary governments that had us by the throat, they wore *red shirts*. Does that mean nothing to you? Have you no sense of patriotism? What's come over you, my girl? What's come over Italy?'

'The colour's all right,' conceded Francesca, 'although I prefer yellow. And perhaps green. Like the Racing Club's colours. It's the cut.'

'Cut?'

'Of the shirts. They look like sacks.'

'They *are* sacks. That is all that poor people can afford.'

'The material could certainly do with improvement. But it's not so much the material, it's the cut. The style.'

'Ah, we're back to that, are we? Fashion.'

'The club people wear vests.'

'Well, I wear a vest, don't I? Only I keep it under my shirt.'

'But, really, it's the cut of the trousers. And, yes, Grandfather, I *have* noticed: you wear trousers too. But these are racing trousers.'

'My trousers are *honest* trousers. They're the trousers of an honest working man.'

'But shorts are coming in. I prefer shorts.'

'And I know why,' retorted Giuseppi. 'It's because you like to see the men's big, hairy thighs.'

'Giuseppi!' said Maria, shocked. 'You shouldn't go putting ideas into her head!'

'I'm not putting ideas into her head,' said Giuseppi. 'I'm just recognizing that they're there.'

'Francesca, will you go inside? There is something I want to say to your grandfather.'

'I like the socks, too,' said Francesca, over her shoulder, as she retreated.

'Giuseppi –'

'I know, I know. I shouldn't go on at her. Well, I wouldn't, only – only it worries me. Not the clothes. What do I know about clothes? One shirt is pretty much like another as far as I am concerned. Nor the bicycles. Bicycles are all right in the right hands, the hands of those Reds, for example, when they're being put to a good purpose. No, it's not that. It's just that I don't like her hanging around the army.'

'Well, you know why she does that, don't you?'

'Of course, I know!'

'It's her father. She's missing him.'

'I know that, too. Don't forget, I'm the one who told him not to.'

'Yes, but you told him in such a way as to put his back up. You only made him more determined.'

'Julia should have talked him out of it.'

'She tried to.'

'That a daughter of mine should be so stupid as to marry a man going into the army!'

'What else was there for him to do? You said yourself that there were not the jobs to be found here.'

'Well, he could have gone to Milan, couldn't he?'

'No. There aren't jobs there, either. What he did made sense. He would sign on for three years and then he would be able to come out with a gratuity. He would come back here and start up a bicycle shop. What's wrong with that?'

'Nothing. Provided you don't get a bullet through your head meanwhile.'

'At least he was doing *something*. He wasn't just hanging around, like Gianni or Ronaldo. You wouldn't have liked that, would you?'

'It's all wrong. That these boys should have no work to go to when they leave school. It's the system that's wrong.'

'Oh, yes, the system! With you it's always the system that's wrong.'

'Well, it is!'

'And while we're waiting for that to change, we'll all die of old age. At least Marcello had the guts to do something.'

Francesca came out again.

'Jalila is here,' she informed her grandfather.

'And that's another thing,' said Giuseppi.

Chapter Three

An Arab woman came through the door from the kitchen holding two small children by the hands.

'It's not come again,' she said to Giuseppi, 'although they swore it would be here by Tuesday. I'll have to go to the office again.'

'I'll come with you this time,' said Giuseppi.

'Would you? They don't listen to me.'

'They'll listen to *me*,' said Giuseppi fiercely.

Her eyes took in Chantale sitting at the table.

'*Buon giorno*, Signora,' she said politely.

'*Buon giorno!*'

Chantale put her hand out and touched the children gently on their cheeks.

'*Buon giorno*, little ones!' she said.

'*Buon giorno*, Signora,' said the little girl, and then came up to Chantale and stood beside her looking up at her with wide dark eyes.

The mother hesitated. 'And you, Signora, are not from Italy?'

'From Morocco,' said Chantale.

The woman looked puzzled. 'And your husband?'

'My fiancé,' said Chantale, who increasingly found herself liking the description.

'English,' said Seymour.

'Ah, English,' murmured the Arab woman. 'You are visitors, then?'

'On holiday,' said Chantale.

'On holiday? How nice! Tonio always said that when he

got back to Naples, we would have a holiday. The four of us. But . . .' She shrugged.

'He was going to go back to his old job,' said Giuseppi, 'at the baker's.'

'But then he hoped to move on from there,' said the Arab woman. 'He wanted to start up on his own. With the gratuity.'

'You'd think they'd give you that at least,' said Giuseppi. 'How do they think you're going to manage?'

The woman shrugged again. 'Some of it may come, they say. But the pension's the thing. When it's gone through. And, meanwhile, people are kind. Giovanni's kind. He gives me work to do cleaning.'

'That's all very well,' said Giuseppi. 'But you've got entitlements. As the widow of an Italian soldier. A pension, for instance. It wouldn't be a lot, but it would be enough to keep you going. You would have thought that they would have got that worked out by now. But they just sit on their backsides all day doing nothing. I'll go down there and see if I can get them moving.'

'Not too fierce, not too fierce, I beg of you,' said the Arab woman, shrinking.

'Get Rinaldo to go with you!' called Maria from the kitchen. 'He's got some pull with the Mayor.'

'That's not a bad idea,' conceded Giuseppi. 'It will look more official that way. They won't listen to a woman on her own, but if it's a deputation –'

'And Pietro,' called Maria.

'Pietro! Right! Don't worry, my dear,' he said to the Arab woman. 'You're not on your own. There are people here who'll show some solidarity.'

The little girl couldn't take her eyes off Chantale.

'You have pretty hair, Signora,' she said shyly.

'Thank you.'

'But you shouldn't show it,' she said.

'In Italy you can show it,' said Francesca.

'Yes, you can,' said Chantale. 'It's all right here. But I know what you mean. In my country, where I come from, a woman can't show it, either.'

'Do you come from Tripoli?' asked the little girl.

'Tripoli? No. Tangier.'

'Tangier.' The little girl tried it out.

Giuseppi took her hand in his.

'Let's go into the kitchen, Atiya,' he said, 'and see if Maria can find you something. And after that I'll go down to the market and talk to Rinaldo and Pietro.'

'Don't talk too long!' called Maria. 'Remember, you're supposed to be going to the office with Jalila.'

'I won't talk too long.'

'You will, if you get talking politics.'

'Do I ever talk politics?' Giuseppi appealed to the world at large.

The Arab woman lingered.

'And your family, Signora,' she said to Chantale, 'are they in England? Or in Morocco?'

'Morocco.'

'But you live in England?'

'Yes.'

'Of course, you have your husband's family there. But it is not the same thing. My husband's family have been kind to me, very kind. But it is not quite the same thing. I always feel, still feel, a stranger.'

'But your children won't feel like that,' said Chantale.

'I hope not. I hope not. Tonio always said, if anything should happen to me, take them back to Italy. My family will look after them. They are not rich but in Italy every-one is more rich than they are in Libya. It will be better for them to grow up there. These things matter. So I brought them here. But sometimes I wonder if I have done right.'

They had intended to go up on the heights above the town and look down on the full stretch of the bay, but already it was too hot and they decided to postpone it until the evening. Instead, they wandered through the dark, narrow but cool streets of the old town, where the women stood outside the *bassi*, the small open-fronted shops, which also

34

served as living quarters, combing their hair. The men were at work at their various crafts inside: but occasionally as you went past you could see that the family bed was still occupied, often by five or six small children and sometimes an older grandmother or grandfather. You wondered how the husband and wife managed to squeeze in.

There were often the remains of meals thrown casually into the streets where, later, they might be swept up by the dust carts. Or they might not, and a safer bet was that the still edible bits would be devoured by the starving cats and dogs with which the neighbourhood abounded.

Or, possibly, by the goats. At this hour in the morning the streets were full of them. They would come through the Posillipo tunnel, leaving an incredible stink behind them, and then fan out in herds to their regular beats. They wound in and out of the cats and pedestrians and some-times into the *bassi*. When they came to the abode of a customer a goat would walk in, followed by the goatherd, while her companions lay down in the street, walk up the stairs and stop outside the right door, where she would be milked by the goatherd. Then she would walk sedately down the stairs and out on to the street again. For a cou-ple of hours in the morning they would be everywhere; and then, suddenly, they would be gone, back down the tunnel and out on to the slopes of the hills to browse on the sparse grass.

Like so much else in Naples they were such an accus-tomed part of life as to become invisible.

Like, for example, the *cabalisti* who were to be found in almost every street.

Cabalisti? Magicians? It took Seymour a while to work it out. At last he got it. A magician who specialized in num-bers. And in particular the numbers that came up in lot-teries. Forecasting the winner was an industry in Naples. Every newspaper devoted several columns to advertise-ments from tipsters, offering for a few pence to supply winning numbers. Posters were plastered in every street directing you to the premises of the local cabbalists. Every café, every bar, had a Smorfia, the lottery dictionary he had come across earlier, giving a numbered value to any event that could happen.

On an impulse Seymour went into one of the cabbalists.

'Age?' said the *cabalista*, before Seymour had even opened his mouth.

'Thirty-one. But –'

'Height?'

'Look –'

'Six feet, I would say. That's good, that's promising. But we need to be more precise than that. Six feet? Or six feet one? Or five eleven and a half?'

'Never mind about that –'

'But it does matter. It could make all the difference. There are lots of people who are six feet. Well, not many in Naples, in fact, and there you have an advantage. But there will be others. Cannot you be more precise?'

'Listen, I don't want to be precise. Or, at least, I do, but about something else.'

'My system can take in anything,' said the *cabalista*. 'I am not like the others.'

'Can it take in this?' said Seymour, laying the ticket he had taken from Scampion's pocket in front of him.

'That's no good!' said the *cabalista* disgustedly. 'You've already got one.'

'What can you tell me about it?'

'Tell you about it? There's nothing worth telling you. It's useless.'

'Because the time has expired?'

'Yes.'

'What else can you tell me?'

'The numbers?' The *cabalista* turned the ticket over.

'Very dull,' he said. 'It's just using the Smorfia. Now, if he had used my system –'

'Have you got a Smorfia?'

'Of course.'

'Can you decode these numbers for me?'

'Yes.'

He looked in his book.

'It's an address. I think. That number is the street. And that will be the number of the house . . . Hello, that's not much of a number . . . Oh, I know what this will be.'

He looked triumphantly at Seymour.

'Yes?'

'It's the Hospital.'

'The Hospital?'

'The Foundling Hospital. One of the most important institutions in Naples. About half the population have some connection or other with it.'

'Foundling?'

'There are a lot of foundlings in Naples.'

'I see.'

The *cabalista* handed the ticket back to Seymour.

'Does that help you?'

'Perhaps it does. Up to a point.'

'You were looking for a place?'

'A person, rather.'

'Ah, well, even there the numbers will help. Each child who is taken in is given a number. It is put on a label around the child's neck. And, of course, they keep a record of it. Let me have a look at that ticket again.'

He studied it.

'I don't understand this number,' he said. 'Perhaps that will be the personal number, the number on its label.'

'Would – would a person keep it?'

'Oh, yes!' said the *cabalista*, affronted. 'It's a good number. And it's a personal one. It would be special to its owner. Very special. And there could be no confusion, you see. No one else would have it. If it was just a house number, other people could live in the house. Suppose it was a big block of apartments, say. There could be hundreds with the same number. But this number would be unique to you. So it's your lucky number.'

'One you would bet with?'

'Certainly. I would always encourage a client to use that number if he had one.'

* * *

37

'A magician?' said Chantale incredulously.

'Yes. A particular sort of magician. One specializing in numbers.'

'Oh, yes?' said Chantale, even more doubtfully.

'The numbers that turn up in the lotteries. They forecast the winners. They're very popular in Naples.'

'Well, yes, they would be.'

'There's a book, too.'

'A book?'

'Yes. It gives a numbered value for anything that happens and then you can use that number in the lottery.'

'I see. Yes. A magical Book of Numbers?'

'That's right.'

'And you've been ... you've been studying this book?'

'That's right, yes.'

'In your work?'

'Yes.'

'So you say.'

'I do say.'

He explained about the ticket.

'So, naturally, you went at once to this book for guidance?'

'Well, yes.'

'Darling, are you sure you're on top of this case?'

'It sounds a bit potty, I know,' said Seymour defensively.

'It does, yes.'

'But they're all like this. Neapolitans, I mean. It's to do with the betting. They're obsessed with numbers. Crazy about them.'

'And is there any need,' said Chantale, 'for you to join them?'

'So it's given you an address?' said Chantale.

'Yes. A hospital. A hospital for foundlings.'

'And you want us to go there?'

'Yes. It's one of the great sights of Naples, apparently.'

'Do you know,' said Chantale, 'I was planning to see some of the other sights of Naples today. The Castel

38

dell'Ovo, for example. Or perhaps San Martino. The Palazzo, maybe. Or the harbour. Or even – as I thought you were going to show me last night – the view of the bay from Posillipo. But not, actually, a hospital for foundlings.'

'It's a very important institution in Naples, apparently.'

'Yes. I'm sure.'

'We needn't spend hours there,' said Seymour, placatorily.

'We needn't spend any time there at all,' said Chantale.

The huge iron gates of the Hospital were open because it was the feast of the Annunciation, one of the days on which the public was allowed to enter. As Seymour and Chantale approached the gates they saw a notice saying 'Closed'; however this did not refer to the gates or the institution but to a small hole originally about eight inches square but now barred up. Through this hole foundlings were once passed, usually at night, by their mothers to a nun on duty inside. This constituted entry to the institution and guaranteed anonymity. The practice had to be abandoned, however, because attempts were continually being made to thrust large children through. Nowadays, they learned, the child was carried through the door and laid more tenderly in the nun's arms.

The admission was recorded in a large book of forms, each page being devoted to a separate child, and it was at this point that the child was given a number. Alongside it would be a note of the date and the circumstances – for example, '267: 3rd day of June, 1903' – together with a short description, focusing on any distinguishing marks, and listing any items included with the child. Often the children came with a holy, protective amulet. Such property was always kept, together with the garments, if any, that the child had come in. It was a way, said the nun on duty, of establishing the identity later, if that should be required. The child was given new garments and taken at once into the chapel to be baptised.

It was usually given the name of the saint of the day and for surname the name of the Governor of the Hospital for the current year. The last practice had been discarded, however, owing to unfortunate interpretations, and a new practice introduced, that of calling any child admitted 'Esposito', abandoned. That, too, had now been discarded, because it was felt to point a shameful finger at a person's origins.

Not too shameful a finger, thought Seymour, since so many people in Naples appeared to have Esposito as a surname and seemed prepared to use it happily. About every other shop bore the name proudly on its front. A more practical reason probably was the difficulty of distinguishing between so many. With so many Espositos, which was the one you wanted? This was particularly important to the army, most of whose recruits were named Esposito.

The number on Scampion's lottery ticket referred to a girl foundling who had been admitted to the Hospital on 27th March 1880. She had been given the name Margareta, after the saint of the day, together with the universal Esposito. Margareta Esposito was, then, the person whose identity mattered so much to the purchaser of the ticket that he or she had used it as their special number for betting.

And what had happened to her? asked Seymour. Was she still at the Hospital?'

'Oh, no,' said the nun, consulting her records: she had left when she was thirteen.

What to do? asked Seymour.

'Probably marry,' thought the nun. Their girls were much sought after as wives. They were educated, well trained, and disciplined. And religious, of course. All qualities thought desirable in a wife.

Some, however, would go on to a trade, for which, again, they were much sought after, on the grounds that they had been brought up to work hard and not answer back.

And this one, this Margareta Esposito, had she left to marry or to take up a trade?

The nun consulted her records, and then frowned. On this one, she said, she would have to consult Sister

40

Geneviève. Who would at the moment, she guessed, be in the chapel.

A choir was practising in the chapel when they went in. They were singing rather beautifully.

Three nuns were conducting the practice. One was actually a member of the choir and was leading it. Another was conducting. A third, much older than the other two, so old that she was bent down double, and had to sit down to one side, was offering a kind of general supervision. This was Sister Geneviève. She had, said the nun who had brought them in, herself conducted the choir for many years, but recently, as infirmity grew, she had taken to playing a more minor part. It was Sister Geneviève, said the nun, who had been in charge of the choir at the time Margareta Esposito had been one of its leading members.

'Oh, yes,' she said brightly, 'I remember Margareta. What a beautiful voice she had! So beautiful that the Pietà came after her. You know about the Pietà, of course? No? Well, it is Vivaldi's church. At Venice. An institution, like ours, for foundlings, and he was Director of Music there. Goodness, how I would have liked to have been there when he was! He wrote music especially for them. They were all girls, of course, and so good!

'Even after he died, the musical tradition continued. But in late years they were not always altogether scrupulous. When they heard of an outstanding singer in a place like ours they would tempt her away. And they tempted Margareta. We resisted, of course, but they had friends in high places and we were not able to prevail against them. So Margareta left us before we had really had the benefit of her remarkable voice. It *was* a remarkable voice. I can still hear it . . .'

She closed her eyes.

'I can still hear it in my head. Such a pity that she left! From all points of view, hers as much as our own. For while she benefited from the Pietà, of course – who could not benefit? – she became more worldly. She lost the simple faith that we had given her, lost, perhaps, the love and respect with which we surrounded her. She became, so I

41

have heard, wilder, less reconciled. It is a difficult time for girls, those years between fifteen and eighteen, and if there are not good people at hand, they can go astray.'

'And Margareta Esposito went astray?' asked Seymour.

'Very much so.' Sister Geneviève sighed. 'She became an opera singer.'

'An opera singer? Well, that's rather good, isn't it?'

'Some would think so, but ... Many, perhaps, would think so,' conceded Sister Geneviève despite herself. 'And certainly she had the voice for it. When she was with us her voice was still young and I thought we could develop it in terms of church music. And there was always that timbre there, and I suppose that as she grew older, her voice changed and she lost some of the early purity and gained in the capacity to produce deeper, richer notes. Colour – she always had plenty of colour. Too much, perhaps. I tried to discipline it out of her, but I don't think the Pietà were as successful. But who am I to say? Her voice changed, that was all. And perhaps she changed with it.

'Anyway, she left the Pietà. They lost her voice but gained in reputation, and Margareta went on to do very well.'

'She still sings?'

'Not now. She married, I think. Well, that is good, is God's will for some of us. But I think it was a loss. A loss to God. Such a talent should have been used for God's purposes. But who am I to say that it was not? I do not like opera myself, but it gives pleasure to so many that it cannot be altogether evil. Maybe God thought she could serve Him best in that way. Who knows?'

'And you have lost track of her now?' asked Seymour.

'I do not follow the opera,' said Sister Geneviève, 'and, in any case, she no longer sings. But I can tell you one thing. She has not altogether forgotten us. Sometimes our daughters come back. Years later, sometimes. And when they do, they sometimes take away their things. Those little things they brought with them when they were admitted as a baby, things that speak to them, perhaps, of the mother they never knew. An amulet say, or a charm. Sometimes, too, they take away the label that they were given when they entered and which they kept through all the time they were here – something to remind them, perhaps, of us, or, more probably, of the child they were once and which they are no longer. I looked once to see if Margareta had come back. She had. And she had taken away her things. And her label.'

As they were coming back from the Hospital they went past the Porta Capuana, which was as usual bustling with people, animals, carts, and trade of all kinds. You could hear it as you approached: the bleating, whinnying and people talking at top volume, gesticulating as they did so. In several places tables had come together to form a kind of impromptu café, and in one of these they saw Giuseppi, contributing his quota to the noise.

And right beside him, arms akimbo, in exactly the pose of her grandmother and, no doubt, the other long-suffering women of Naples, was Francesca.

'Grandmother says: what about the office?'

Giuseppi waved a dismissive hand.

'And Jalila,' persisted Francesca.

'Later, later,' said Giuseppi, continuing with his conversation.

'You *promised*,' said Francesca. 'You said you would go to the office with Jalila.'

'Well, I will. In a bit.'

'Grandmother says you won't have time to do it before lunch.'

Giuseppi waved an airy hand.

'Yes, I will,' he said.

'And that you won't get lunch unless you've done it.'

This stopped Giuseppi in mid-flow.

'There's plenty of time,' he protested.

'And she meant it,' said Francesca implacably.

'Look, I've said I will –'

'It will be too late. You know what they're like. They'll

43

be closing early for lunch. And then Jalila will be going without money for another day. And It Will Be Your Fault.'

Giuseppi began to get up, still talking.

'And Rinaldo and Pietro,' said Francesca.

'What?' said the other two men at the table.

'That's the point of it,' said Francesca. 'The point of him talking to you. To get you to go with him.'

'Go where?' said one of the men, astonished.

'To the office. To get them to pay Jalila her pension.'

'I was coming to that!' protested Giuseppi.

'Jalila?'

'Yes. Tonio's widow. She's had nothing so far.'

'That's not right!'

'It's an injustice.'

'And Grandmother said you were just the men to put it right. You were to go with Grandfather. Otherwise he would wander off the point.'

The men laughed.

'It's true, Giuseppi!'

'And so he was to ask you to come with him.'

'Well, I don't mind that. This is the widow of an Italian soldier, and she's got her rights. Not only that, she's one of ours. In a manner of speaking.'

'Even if she's an Arab,' said the other man.

Seymour and Chantale were still having lunch when Giuseppi returned.

'Well,' said Maria, 'did you get it?'

'Yes. It will start next week.'

'That's no good. They'll have found a reason why it shouldn't by then.'

'And meanwhile,' said Giuseppi, 'they're paying her some money in advance.'

'Next week too?'

Giuseppi put his hand in his pocket and produced some notes.

'Now,' he said. 'That was Pietro's idea. He and Rinaldo insisted on it.'

'I suppose it's something,' said Maria grudgingly. 'But I'll believe that about the pension starting when I see it.'

'Oh, it will start,' said Giuseppi confidently. 'You see, Rinaldo told them that Our Friends held an interest.'

'You told them *that*?'

'Yes.'

'But what happens when they find out?'

'Rinaldo's going to have a word with them tonight.'

'With Our Friends?'

'That's right.'

'I don't like that,' said Maria.

'Well, I don't like it, either. But it was the best we could do in the circumstances. Look, you've no idea what it takes to shift these bureaucrats. Unless you put the fear of God into them, they won't do anything.'

'All the same –'

'It will be all right. Rinaldo is going to speak to them. Tonight. They'll do it as a favour.'

'And what favour will they ask for in return?'

'Look, it will be as a general favour. They won't be asking for anything particular in return.'

'Well, if they do – *when* they do – just tell me about it, will you? I don't want you getting mixed up in anything like that.'

'Look, I've always stood out against that sort of thing, haven't I? Refused to pay protection? Turned them away when they came round asking for something?'

'Yes, but now you haven't. You've asked *them* for something.'

'You wanted me to get the money for Jalila, didn't you?'

'Not like this. Not in this way.'

'You want me to go back and tell Rinaldo that it's all off?'

'I just don't want us to have too much to do with the Camorra, that's all.'

'It's not as easy as that,' Giuseppi complained, after Maria had gone back into the kitchen. 'You can't get anything done in Naples unless you go through the Camorra. Well,

45

you don't even need to go through them. You just need to know that you have their support. Or, at least, that they're not against it. And they're not usually against seeing that people get their dues. Ordinary people, that is. I mean, it would be stupid of them, wouldn't it? It could put people's backs up. And they're usually on the side of the poor. But you've got to go about it in the right way. Make sure that what you want doesn't clash with something that they've got in mind. Often you've just got to let them know. Just mention it. That's what Rinaldo's doing tonight. Not asking for anything, just mentioning it. What's wrong with that? And, anyway, she herself told me to bring him in on it, didn't she?'

He poured himself a glass of wine.

'The thing is, you see, it's not entirely straightforward. Jalila's being an Arab, you see. I mean, in the ordinary way, if it was just the widow of a soldier, and he was one of ours, there'd be no problem. But her being an Arab. Look, it doesn't matter to me, her being an Arab. She's just Tonio's widow, as far as I'm concerned.

'Tonio's my brother's son. Born the same year as our Marcello. The two of them were always close, always did things together. Enlisted together. The fools! Well, there wasn't much else for them to do round here. Anyway, they went into the army together and were sent out to Libya together.

'Only Tonio got himself killed. But not before he had had time to marry and have children. So when he died there was a question of what to do with the wife and kids. Well, you would have thought that the best thing would be for her family to look after them. But there were problems about that, apparently, and Marcello said that Tonio had laid it upon him as a sacred trust to see that they were provided for.

'Well, I don't know how he thought he was going to do that on a private's pay but what he did was to send her home to my brother's family. Well, of course, they agreed to take her. It was only right, her being their son's wife. But my brother is older than I am, and so is my sister-in-law, and her health is none too good. It's a lot to take on. Of course, we do what we can to help, but it's not easy. People look at Jalila all the time, you know, and they wonder. What is she doing here?

'But that's war for you. You go off with your flags flying and everyone cheering and all the girls around your neck. But then the casualties begin to come home. And, of course, some, like Tonio, don't come home at all. And then you know what war is. And you begin to wonder, if you've not wondered before, what the hell Italy is doing out there.

'Liberating people and opening up trade, they say. But it's not our people who are liberated, and it's not the ordinary men who benefit from the trade. It's the banks and the big people. And the small ones, like Tonio, are the ones who get hit by the bullets.'

Chapter Four

Down the street came the cyclists, pedalling furiously:
three out in front, then several in a bunch, and, finally,
some solitary ones straggling behind them. The scattered
crowd raised a cheer. And there ahead of them was Porta
Capuana with the crowded thoroughfares on either side
and a great crush of people coming and going.

The Porta was the announced finishing point, but the
racers, mercifully, stopped some hundred yards short,
where two officials in the colours of the Racing Club of
Naples, surrounded by a herd of urchins, were furiously
waving flags. Two or three other men in the Club's colours
were intercepting the riders as they came in and noting
down their times and numbers on clipboards.

'Are you the last, Umberto?'

'Me?' affecting affront. 'No, there are others behind me.'

And, indeed, one or two fresh riders, or, possibly, not
quite so fresh, were just coming into view.

'That last hill was a killer!' said one, panting.

'You've got to take it fast,' someone advised him.

'What do you think I was doing?'

'Maybe we ought to make the last bit downhill next
time.'

'What, and have a big pile-up at the end?'

'It would add something.'

'A dozen people with their necks broken?'

'You know what I mean. A bit of extra excitement.'

'There's enough excitement as there is. And suppose
some daft bugger runs in front?'

'He could run out now.'

'Yes, but if we are all going that much faster, and we were all in a bunch at the end, it could cause mayhem!'

At the moment the racers had a hundred yards or so to slow to a stop before they ran into the great stone wall of the Porta. Even so, there was much skidding of bicycles at the last moment.

'Darling, you were tremendous!' said a woman's voice among the skids.

'I was, wasn't I?'

'And your shorts, dear, are even more tremendous.'

'I did what you said. Sat down in the water with them on to shrink them.'

'It worked perfectly. Skintight, and shows everything off to advantage.'

'Not too tight? I thought I heard a split at one point.'

'Let me look. Oh, good heavens! There's a great tear and everything's dangling out!'

'Jesus!'

'What was that you were saying about adding to the excitement?'

'Christ, let me have a towel, somebody!'

'She's having you on, Vincente,' someone advised.

'Is she? Luisa, you bitch!'

'Luisa,' said Richards, 'can I introduce you to a colleague of mine? This is Seymour. Seymour, this is the Marchesa.'

'So I guessed. Delighted to meet you, Marchesa.'

'And you speak Italian? Why, this is a strange thing! The Foreign Office don't usually send people here who can speak Italian.'

'He is not Foreign Office. He's here on holiday. With his fiancée.'

'Ah? And what have you done with your fiancée, Mr Seymour? Where is she?'

'Over here,' said Chantale. 'Keeping out of the way.'

'Advisedly. I have noticed that when they cross the finishing line, the first thing they do is throw their arms round the nearest woman. I have never been able to make out whether it is the release of heaving passion temporarily bridled for the length of the race or because otherwise they would fall off. The latter, I suspect. Of course all these under-age girls love it. But you and I, Signorina, being more chaste, or, at any rate, more mature, can do without it.'

'In my case, it's chaste, Marchesa,' declared Chantale.

'Of course. And an Englishwoman's natural reserve. But then, you are not an Englishwoman, are you, Signorina? Where are you from? Libya?'

'Morocco.'

'Ah, then, our gallant soldiers will still have some way to go even when they get to Libya, if they want to find someone like you. They will just have to pedal further, that's all. Which they may well be prepared to do, of course, if they see someone like you at the end of the road. However, I am forgetting. The French have got there first. Closely followed, it would appear, by the British.'

'Seymour is a policeman,' said Richards. 'We thought that while he was here he might take a look at that Scampion business.'

'It's taken them long enough to send someone,' said the Marchesa. And is he up to the job? said her look of cool appraisal.

'I would appreciate a private word with you, Marchesa,' said Seymour.

'No words are private in Naples,' said the Marchesa, 'but you can try. I shall be in the San Stefano at lunchtime.'

'You're supposed to be having lunch with me,' complained Vincente.

'Why, so I am. Bring your fiancée along, Mr Seymour, and she and Vincente can entertain each other while we talk. Vincente is my cousin, Signorina, and quite safe. That is, he's entirely biddable. I find that it is not what men have in mind that is significant – they all have the same thing in mind – but whether they'll do what they're told. Vincente will always do what he is told.'

'Luisa, you bitch!' said Vincente.

'The San Stefano at one,' said the Marchesa.

* * *

50

The cyclists began to wheel their bicycles away to the square in front of the Palazzo Reale where they congregated before and after the races.

'My last time,' one of them said to Vincente. 'I'm off to Libya next week.'

'Lucky sod!' said Vincente.

The other man looked at him curiously.

'Your turn never comes up, Vincente, does it?'

'I know, Umberto. It's not for want of reminding. I remind them every time.'

'I'm sure.'

'But you're right. I'm beginning to think it can't be an accident. I think my father must have fixed it.'

'You think he doesn't want you to go?'

'I think my mother doesn't want me to go. And she can wrap my father around her little finger.'

'Can't you bypass them somehow?'

'I thought of speaking to Alessandro, Luisa's husband. He's well up in Rome. I would ask Luisa to speak to him, only she says she doesn't want to lose her little cousin just yet. Not until another good dancer comes along. "Listen, Luisa," I say, "there are dozens of good dancers among the officers." "But they're all so sweaty," she says. "It's all the bicycling they do. And, while we're on the subject, Vincente, can I just drop a hint?" "I always have a shower when I get back to the barracks after racing," I say. "Yes, but before you get back to barracks –"'

'That's unreasonable!' said Umberto.

'That's what I tell her, but she waves it away.'

Umberto laughed. 'She's a character, isn't she? A real character!'

'She's all right,' Vincente conceded. 'It's just that she's a bit out of place down here. "That's why I can't let you go and get yourself killed just yet, Vincente," she says. "You're the one thing I've got to remind me of Rome. Without you I would dwindle away. Just disappear." I've tried it – tried getting her to speak to Alessandro. But somehow it never works. She always slips away somehow. "I'm the wrong

51

person," she says. "I never speak to my husband, and in the days when I did, he never listened to me."'

'Well, keep trying,' said Umberto, wheeling his bicycle away.

'They are *so* beautiful,' sighed Francesca.

'If I had as much money as they have, I would be beautiful, too,' said Giorgio.

'Money isn't everything,' said Francesca.

'Maybe, but it means you can buy a good bicycle.'

'If things work out the way you want,' said Francesca kindly, 'you *will* be able to buy a good bicycle.'

'Yes, but it will take so long! Another eighteen months before I can enlist, then three years in the ranks, and only then can I come home. And buy a bicycle.'

'And marry,' sighed Francesca. 'I will still be waiting for you, Giorgio.'

'I'll probably get shot,' said Giorgio gloomily.

Francesca laid her hand on his arm.

'Do not say that, Giorgio. Do not ever say that. Even in jest.'

'Maybe I won't die,' said Giorgio, pleased with the effect he had produced.

Seymour went over to one of the race officials who was just packing up.

'Another successful event,' he said.

'It was, wasn't it?' agreed the man.

'The loss of that poor Englishman who was killed doesn't seem to have affected things.'

'No, it hasn't. Of course, other people stepped in. Vincente, for example. These days, though, it mostly runs itself.'

'Ah, you say that. But without the help of devoted people like you –'

'Oh, I don't know. There would be others. I used to race myself, you know. But then I had an injury.'

'It's good of you to stay involved.'

'I'd go mad, otherwise. I was about to be posted but then, when the injury happened, of course I couldn't go. I've just been hanging around here!'

'I was shocked when I heard about the Englishman. Stabbed! In broad daylight! I didn't realize that sort of thing happened down here.'

'Well, it does. There are plenty of people in the back streets who are a bit too ready with a knife.'

'But why? He doesn't seem to have been the sort of chap who would bring a thing like that upon himself.'

'Well, no.'

'I wondered if it was anything to do with the racing?'

'I don't think so. Why should it be?'

'Well, look, I'm a stranger here so I wouldn't know. But there's a lot of betting, isn't there? And I wondered if that could be something to do with it?'

'Well, it could, to be honest. There *is* a lot of betting, although I didn't notice there was that much on us. But where there is betting, there is usually the Camorra. And if there was something going on, they might be ready to use their knives.'

'Who would know about this? About the betting world, I mean? The lottery is municipal, isn't it? We have private bookmakers at home.'

'Well, we don't exactly have bookmakers, but just about every bar in Naples has a finger in the pie. You could try asking in one of them. But I'll tell you what.' The man laughed. 'The person to ask is Father Pepito.'

'Father Pepito?'

'Yes. He has a parish just outside Naples. Or, at least, he did have until they caught up with him. They found that there was an obscure lottery office in a little village and every week a considerable sum was being paid out in winnings. They looked into it and found that the winner was always the same man, a priest.

'He was a man of exemplary piety and spent all his winnings on good causes, the Church, charities, gifts to the poor. Never on himself. So people said, well, look, maybe the Madonna helps him. Gives him the tips in a dream. She might do that if it was all for the poor.

'And his bosses in the Church, the Cardinal himself, so they say, said, well, look, he's only doing good, and, certainly, the people he helps could do with the money. The Church is glad of the money. And then charities, well, they're all beyond reproach. Of course, we've got to be sure that it's all above board. Well, they checked, and everything *was* above board. So they said, well, okay, you can go on. But keep it decent. And how do you do it, by the way?

'Well, he said, before I became a priest I was a professor. At Salerno University. I was a mathematician and interested in probability theory. And I worked out this system . . .

'Well, of course, they couldn't leave it like that and wanted to know more. But he wouldn't tell them. No, he said, I'm using it for God's purposes and that ought to be enough for you. But it wasn't enough for the people in the tax office and they began asking questions.

'Well, I don't know what they found, but one day Father Pepito got called in by the bishop. I don't know what was said but after that Father Pepito stopped placing bets. I think a deal was struck with the tax authorities. They would take no action if the betting stopped and the bishop kept an eye on him. Anyway, after that, Father Pepito stopped betting. He was transferred to another church, one closer to the city, where the bishop could see what he was doing, and concentrated on his duties as priest.

'But if you need to know anything about betting in Naples, he's the man I suggest you go to.'

When, later, Seymour and Chantale got to the San Stefano, they found Vincente there but no Marchesa.

'She's awful!' Vincente said. 'She always does this!'

'Doesn't turn up?'

'Oh, she turns up. Eventually. But late. Always late! But at least *you* are here, Signorina,' he said, kissing Chantale's hand, which Chantale liked but Seymour didn't.

He led them into a large lounge. It was a very high room with shutters over the windows and glass doors which opened on to a little patio with orange trees in pots and small tubbed palm trees. In one corner, behind the orange trees, there was a table and benches.

'This pleases you?' Vincente said to Chantale.

'It seems just right. Cool in the shade but with a little air.'

'Yes. Inside, it is cool but there is no air.'

'Will the Marchesa find us?' asked Seymour.

'Oh, yes. When she gets here,' said Vincente gloomily. He brightened. 'We could have a drink,' he said, 'and put it on her bill. A limoncello, Signorina? They do cocktails here but I don't know that I would recommend them. I think I shall have a beer.'

'A beer for me, too, please,' said Seymour.

Vincente disappeared inside and came back followed by a waiter with a tray on which were the various drinks, together with bowls of pistachio nuts and olives.

'If she leaves it too long, we'll have lunch,' he said. 'We'll put that on her bill, too. She'll complain but she's got pots of money. Her husband, Alessandro, is a banker. Not a lot of it comes my way, though, I have to say.'

'And your cousin has been banished here, I gather,' said Seymour.

'Banished?' said Chantale. 'To Naples?'

Vincente nodded. 'Alessandro insisted that she leave Rome. It got so bad. But where could she go? She barely knew that there *were* places outside Rome. Milan? But that is where Alessandro does a lot of business and he wasn't having her there. Florence? But that was where she had been before and where it got so awful. Naples was the only place left.'

'Florence was where she met Signor Scampion, wasn't it?'

'He was one of a crowd. The D'Annunzio crowd. When D'Annunzio got thrown out, she was at a loss. Didn't know what to do. Became even wilder.'

'And Scampion?'

'Got wilder, too. They all did.'

'He was banished to Naples, too.'

'Yes, but it was at about that time that he discovered bicycling. It was all the rage. I got myself a bicycle and started to go out every afternoon. We formed a club. That's where Scampion got the idea. It was the same people, really. Army officers. We were all browned off, with nothing to do. Waiting for Libya. So bicycling was a life-saver. Well, then we all got posted down here – it's a transit camp, you see. People on their way to Libya. And then Scampion came along and said, why don't we set up a club here, too? The Racing Club of Naples? And so we did.'

'And you've carried on with it?'

'Yes. I was the obvious man. I'd been helping him do the running. Well, I didn't mind. It gave me something to do. A life-saver for me, too.'

'And it seems to have really taken off,' said Seymour.

'Well, yes, it's proved pretty popular. Of course, we have a big turnover. More people leave after a time. But then new people are always coming, that's the other side of it. So the Club stays much the same size.'

'And mostly army officers?'

'Oh, yes.'

'I just wondered if you took in many members from outside?'

'Well, in principle it's open to anyone. But in practice – well, I suppose it's pretty well all officers. The thing is, you see, we couldn't just have anybody. They've got to be the right sort.'

'And there aren't people of the right sort in Naples?' asked Chantale.

'Not really. You know, Naples is a poor town. Oh, it seems very nice, I know, with the bay and all that. But there's not a lot of money around. There isn't much money in the south as a whole. Southern Italy is very poor. So there aren't, really, people of the right sort.'

'There's a bit of a gap, then, between the Club and the town?'

'There are not many other bicyclists in Naples, if that's what you mean. But I think that they like to see us. For one thing, when we race every Saturday it's a bit of fun for them. The Neapolitans like a spectacle. Besides, well, you know, it's the army. And there's a lot of pride in the army just now. People like to see us. I think, you know, we do a lot of good. Just by showing ourselves. Waving the flag, as it were. Reminds them there's a war on. And the fact that we're off to fight pretty soon, well, I think it has an effect on people.'

The Marchesa swept out on to the patio and paused.

'My dear!' she cried. 'A thousand apologies! I'm late again – I bought a few things and they took so long to wrap them up! Has Vincente been looking after you? I'm sure he has! And are these drinks? I could do with one myself after the morning I've had! Vincente, order a cocktail for me!'

'Well, I could, but are you sure?'

'Why shouldn't I be sure?'

'They don't do very good ones here. And they haven't heard of half of them. If you're hoping for a Fuzzy Bear, I would forget about it.'

'No Fuzzy Bear? Couldn't you show them how, Vincente? I'm sure you could.'

'Well, I could, if they had everything I need.'

'Tell them to send out for things if they haven't got them,' advised the Marchesa.

'It will take ages,' grumbled Vincente, but he went off.

'He fusses,' said the Marchesa, 'but –' she smiled at Chantale – 'he's very biddable. Why don't you go and bid him, my dear?'

Chantale stayed put.

'No? Oh, well . . .' She shrugged. 'He's really quite nice when you get to know him. As I'm sure you would find.'

Chantale studied her glass.

The Marchesa laughed.

'I was just trying to arrange things so that I could have a private tête-à-tête with Mr Seymour. To talk business. *Business*,' she repeated with emphasis.

'*Do* you want to talk business?' Chantale asked Seymour.

'Well . . .'

He was beginning to see that there could be a disadvantage about having Chantale with him.

Chantale got up and stalked away: *not* in the direction Vincente had taken, however.

The Marchesa watched her go, smiling.

'And you really are here to investigate poor Scampion's murder?' she asked, putting her hand on Seymour's arm.

'Yes.'

'Good. It seemed so wrong, somehow, to kill a man like that.'

'Like what, Marchesa?'

'Well, you know. An innocent. That's how I always thought of him. An innocent like you have in those vast Russian novels. Untouched by evil although evil is going on all around him. But he never sees it. We are a terrible lot, you know, the Roman crowd. Or what I think of as the Roman crowd, although I suppose that when Scampion got to know us we were the Florence crowd. But Florence is just a suburb of Rome, anyway. Or it was when D'Annunzio was there.'

'You know, Marchesa, I never knew Scampion. And, of course, I never knew "the Roman crowd". But when you speak of them I think I know what you mean. And from what I have heard of Scampion I find it hard to see him fitting into that world.'

'Oh, he didn't! Not at all.'

'Then how . . .?'

'I don't quite know. He was already part of it when I arrived. But I have a dreadful feeling . . .'

'Yes?'

'That it was through that awful bicycling. It had just become the rage, you see. All the smart young were doing it. A lot of the young officers were doing it and of course they were all well connected. It could have been through them. Or he could simply have met someone at a party. There were plenty of those. Anyway, he got to know D'Annunzio and after that he was simply carried away. On the crest of a bicycle, you might say.'

'D'Annunzio was an enthusiast for bicycling?'

'No, no. At least, not actively. He liked to watch the young officers, with their over-developed thighs, but to watch was about all he wanted. I think he was afraid he might fall off. He wasn't bothered about hurting himself but he *was* afraid he might look ridiculous. He couldn't bear to appear ridiculous. No, riding horses was more his line. He was a divine horseman. Oh, and aeroplanes. He liked driving aeroplanes. Anything that smacked of the cavalry. *Not* bicycles, however. But it could have been at a race that they met. D'Annunzio took a fancy to him and after that he was always in his company.'

'And whirling in a great social whirl?'

'Exactly.' ·

'Meeting people he would not otherwise have met?'

'Yes.'

'And hearing things that he would perhaps not other-wise have heard?'

'Perhaps.'

'You know why I am asking this, Marchesa. There is a story making the rounds that he had heard something that he ought not to have done.'

'I have heard the story.'

'You may even, I think, have been the one who passed it on to the British Embassy?'

'It is possible.'

'Why did you do that?'

The Marchesa was silent for a moment.

Then she said: 'I was angry. Poor little Scampion! What had he done to deserve that? He was an innocent, as I have told you. An innocent always in a world that had turned nasty. Why did they have to kill him?'

'They?'

The Marchesa smiled.

'One hears so many things at parties,' she said.

Vincente reappeared carrying a tray on which was a solitary drink.

'Look, I've done it!' he said triumphantly, setting the glass down on the table beside her.

'Oh, my dear, how clever of you!'

'It was,' he said. 'They hadn't got anything I needed. I had to send round the corner for it. Even for the Martini. Of course, they had a Martini but it wasn't the one I wanted. It makes a difference, you know.'

'I'm sure it does,' said the Marchesa vaguely. 'What would I do without you, dear?'

'Actually,' said Vincente, 'I wanted to talk to you about that. Or at least get you to talk to Alessandro.'

'I never talk to Alessandro,' declared the Marchesa. 'It is a matter of principle. Since he treats me so abominably.'

'Yes, well, couldn't you this once make an exception?'

'Don't be tiresome, Vincente. I know what you want me to ask him and the answer is No. No, to my asking him and No to him doing anything about it. We cannot spare you, Vincente. The family has decided. Your mother would be round every day if he let you go to Libya, and you know he can't bear her. You'll just have to face up to it, Vincente: you can't go to Libya. Now, be a brave man and get back on your bicycle.'

The Marchesa went off to make some more purchases and Vincente walked back with them in the direction of the Porta Capuana. The racers had all moved round now to the piazza in front of the Palazzo Reale and were packing up. Some were riding on their bicycles, other putting their kit into hand-carts.

As they were standing there a file of red-shirted bicyclists rode past at the other end of the piazza.

'Hello!' said one of the racers. 'What are they doing here?'

'It's the Redshirts,' said someone else. 'They're here to bring about the Revolution.'

'They'll have a job! Why don't they stick to bicycling?'

'Or take up racing.'

'Why don't you suggest it, Guglielmo?'

'Challenge them to a race?'

'They're not racers. They'd never do it!'

'Give it a try! They might.'

'They'd be fools if they did.'

'But they *are* fools. They might be tempted.'

'Put one across on the army. Wouldn't that be tempting?'

'They wouldn't stand a chance!'

'I know, but they might not think that.'

'Challenge them, anyway: it might be a bit of fun.'

'There's talk of a race between the Racing Club and the Reds,' said Francesca, as she helped Maria clear away the dishes that evening. 'My money's on the Club.'

'You haven't got any money,' said Giuseppi.

'Giorgio has, and he's putting it on the Racing Club.'

'That boy is going to the bad,' said Giuseppi. 'What is he doing, putting his money on that lot?'

'He thinks they'd win. They're proper cyclists, he says. The Reds are just amateurs.'

'Of course they're amateurs!' said Giuseppi. 'They're honest men who work for a living. Not fancy boys whose fathers top up their pay so that they can go riding about the countryside.'

'What I meant,' said Francesca, 'was that the Club takes cycling seriously. They race every week. Whereas the Reds –'

'– cycle for a purpose,' said Giuseppi. 'And it's a noble purpose. To tell people what an awful government we've got –'

'Don't they know that already?' asked Maria.

'– and what to do about it,' concluded Giuseppi.

'Well, I think they'll get thrashed,' said Francesca.

'People will be putting down their money on this,' said Giuseppi, when Francesca had departed into the kitchen with a pile of dishes.

'Money they haven't got,' said Maria.

'And which they'll lose,' said Giuseppi. 'It's always somebody else who makes the money out of betting.'

'And usually the Camorra,' said Maria.

Giuseppi looked around uneasily.

'Better not say that too loudly,' he said.

'I say what I like,' said Maria, and went off after Francesca.

Chapter Five

'He would have wished you to have them, Giorgio,' said Miss Scampion.

Giorgio seemed stunned.

'How can I ever thank you, Signora?' he muttered.

'It is not me you have to thank,' said Miss Scampion. 'It is my brother.'

'But this . . . this munificence . . .'

He spread his arms, as if overwhelmed.

'I am sure they will mean a lot more to you than they do to me,' said Miss Scampion, pleased.

'They will mean much to me, Signora,' said Giorgio recovering. 'And I shall always treasure them.'

With a sudden unexpected grace he kissed her hand.

'And now at least I won't have to carry them home again,' said Miss Scampion, smiling. 'I brought them in my basket and, really, it made the bicycle quite top-heavy.'

'That is because the weight was all at the front, Signora,' said Giorgio. 'I will make you a little basket that will fit at the back and then you will be able to divide the load.'

'Thank you. I hope, though, that I will not often be carrying so much.'

'They are a treasure, Signora, a treasure!' said Giorgio, his eyes starry.

He took up the magazines tenderly in his arms.

'Do you want some help with reading them?' asked Francesca.

'No, I don't!' said Giorgio indignantly.

He took the pile and sat on a step.

Francesca went off in a huff.

'I am beginning to turn things out, Mr Seymour,' said Miss Scampion. 'I should have done this long ago.'

She collected her bicycle and walked it along the street. The street was too narrow, and too crowded, for her to mount with decorum and ride with safety, but Seymour, whose eyes followed her as she went, saw her reach the broader thoroughfare at the end and ride away.

'A fine pile,' he said to Giorgio, looking at the cycling magazines.

'I could sell them,' said Giorgio, 'but I won't. They are a precious inheritance.'

He showed them to Seymour.

There were two main ones, *Le Vélo* and *L'Auto-Vélo*.

'*Le Vélo* was the first,' said Giorgio. 'It was started in France but now we've got an edition in Italy. The other one, *L'Auto-Vélo*, was also started in France, by Monsieur le Comte de Dion. He is a big industrialist so Giuseppi does not like him. But without him there would be no bicycles. He makes the Dion. He makes motor cars, too, and some say he is going to make aeroplanes. But the bicycles will do for me.'

'I see they're on different coloured paper,' said Seymour.

'Yes, *L'Auto* – it's called *L'Auto* now, the *Vélo* sued, and he had to change the name – is on yellow paper and the *Vélo* on green. There is great rivalry between them, especially now that they've both started sponsoring road races.'

'And teams, too?'

'Yes, and teams.'

'The Racing Club of Naples, Signor Scampion's team, would, then, be in the Dion stable? Since it wears yellow?'

'Yes. The Yellows are more ... how shall I say? ... aristocratic. That is why Giuseppi doesn't like them. But I like them because they are the army's team, and I support the army. One day, when I am old enough, I will join the army and go to Libya and fight. Giuseppi says that the army is for Dion because he sells them most of their equipment. It is a fix, he says. But then, Giuseppi says everything is a fix.'

'Everything *is* a fix,' said Giuseppi, suddenly appearing out of the door. 'And the sooner you find out, young man, the better.'

Giorgio ostentatiously buried himself in a magazine.

'Where did you get these from?' asked Giuseppi. 'You haven't been spending good money on them, have you?'

'Signora Scampion gave them to me,' said Giorgio.

'She should know better. A poor man cannot afford to waste his time on trash like that.'

'They come as a gift,' said Francesca, popping out, 'in memory of her brother.'

Giuseppi sniffed.

Then gasped.

'Francesca! What are you –? What have you –? Maria! Maria!'

'What is it?' said Maria, running out of the kitchen.

Giuseppi gestured towards Francesca. He seemed to have been rendered speechless.

'Francesca, what have you been doing? Oh, Francesca!'

'I have just altered my skirt a little,' muttered Francesca, losing confidence.

'You have made trousers out of it!'

'No, no, just – just stitched the sides together in the middle.'

'But why, Francesca, why?'

'It's handier like this.'

'It's indecent,' said Giuseppi.

'And looks better,' said Francesca.

'The idea! Where do you get these ideas from, Francesca? Your mother is a decent woman – what will she think?'

'What would your father think,' thundered Giuseppi, 'if he learned that his daughter had been making herself into a slut?'

'Go and unstitch – at once!' ordered Maria.

Francesca fled and Chantale and Seymour moved on.

High up in the sacristy, packed in rows along the balcony, but visible to all, were what looked like a collection of travelling-trunks, upholstered in leather and with brass nails, but often with crimson covers of velvet and damask which had faded to russet-gold and amber under the sunlight that filtered in through the windows.

Looking up at them, with glazed, bemused eyes, was a little group of tourists. English, unmistakably, and clearly uncomfortable at the extravagant trappings of a Papist church, but determined to get their money's worth.

'Rum!' pronounced a red-faced, perspiring man, mopping his face with a silk handkerchief. 'That's what I call it!'

Chantale, who had just come into the San Domenico Maggiore with Seymour, was puzzled.

'Rum?' she whispered to Seymour. 'What is this to do with drink?'

'You mean their *bodies* are up there?' said a woman standing beside the leader of the party, whom Seymour now saw to be Richards, on duty for the consulate in Scampion's place. 'Up there? Now?'

'That's right, Mrs Learoyd,' said Richards. 'Those are the coffins of the Aragon rulers of Naples.'

'Coffins?' said the woman, shuddering. 'Those boxes? And they're in them?'

'I imagine so,' said Richards. 'I haven't actually taken a look,' he admitted.

'Isn't it a bit . . . unhygienic?' said Mrs Learoyd.

'Not much risk now, I fancy,' said Richards, 'after all these years. They've been there for centuries.'

'Kings and queens and such?' said Mrs Learoyd. 'Up there?'

'That's right, Mrs Learoyd. The Aragon rulers of Naples at, oh, about the end of the fifteenth century.'

'It's a funny place to put them,' said Mrs Learoyd doubtfully.

'I don't know,' said the man perspiring beside her. 'That way they can keep an eye on things. See what people are up to.'

'The idea of it!' said Mrs Learoyd, shuddering.

'It may have been a temporary measure,' said Richards. 'They were probably put there while their tombs were being prepared. And then the next lot weren't very interested and just left them there.'

'Yes, but you can't do that,' objected Mrs Learoyd. 'Not leave bodies lying around. I mean, suppose we all did it?'

'Well, these days, of course, the city authorities would see that you didn't.'

'You would have thought *someone* would have done something about it. Them being royalty.'

'Perhaps that's why they didn't do something about it?' suggested Richards. 'They didn't want to disturb them. They might think of it as showing a lack of respect for them.'

'Well, I think it's disgusting!' declared Mrs Learoyd. 'The idea of them being up there. Where everyone can see them!'

'Looking down on you,' said her husband.

'It makes me feel quite faint. I want to go back to the hotel.'

'Would you like me to accompany you?' asked Richards, with, Seymour thought, a certain amount of relief.

'No, no, that will not be necessary. We can find our own way, thanks.'

'Thank you very much, Mr Richards,' said a woman politely.

Richards saw Seymour and Chantale standing there and came across.

'I need a drink,' he said. 'Would you care to join me?'

He took them to some tables under a stone archway where it was pleasantly cool.

'A pressed lemon for me, please,' said Chantale.

'A beer for me.'

'I think I'll have a beer, too,' said Richards, signalling to the waiter.

He sat back.

'Phew!' he said. 'Hard work this morning!'

'Do you do it *every* morning?' asked Chantale.

'Not every,' said Richards gloomily, 'although sometimes it feels like it. How are you getting on?'

'With the Scampion business? Well, at any rate, we've made a start. And one or two fresh things have come up.'

'They have? Oh, that's excellent! I was afraid you would find everything buried under a veil of silence.'

'Like this.' Seymour took out the ticket and placed it in front of Richards.

'What is it?'

'A lottery ticket.'

'Oh, yes. Of course. Look, old man, they're not exactly uncommon in Naples.'

'This one was found in Scampion's shorts. The ones he was wearing when he was killed.'

'Really?'

Richards picked it up gingerly. 'Are you sure about that, old man? I wouldn't have said Scampion was the betting sort.'

'This was found by his sister. When she was going through his clothes.'

'Funny!' said Richards. 'I wouldn't have thought he went in for that kind of thing. Dead against it, in fact.'

'Really?'

'Thought it sinful. He was a bit of a child of the manse.'

'I got that impression from his sister, too. But, you see, that makes it all the more interesting.'

'Why he should have it, you mean?'

'Yes. And in his racing shorts.'

Richards handed the ticket back to him. 'Maybe one of his army friends gave it him? He might not have been very interested in betting, but they certainly were!'

'The racing men, you mean?"

'Yes. And one of them might have given it him at the racing. That would account for it being in his shorts.'

'Yes, but *why* would they have given it him? They would surely have known what his attitude to betting was.'

Richards shrugged.

'A bit of a puzzler, I see.' He sipped his beer. 'Of course,' he said, 'they might have given it him *knowing* that he was like that. Expecting him to pass it on. In fact, they might have given it him *to* pass on.'

'*To* pass on?'

'Yes. It's a bit of a Neapolitan habit. Almost a superstition, you might say. Suppose you find yourself somehow with a lottery ticket on your hands unexpectedly. Picked it up, perhaps, in the street, or found it lying on your table when you were having a drink. Well, that's a bit of luck, you haven't earned it. You didn't buy it, did you? So you don't really deserve it. And if you try to benefit from it yourself, well, it might turn out not to be so lucky. It could turn out nasty. So maybe the thing to do is get rid of it. Pass it on. But if you pass it on to a friend, that might not be very friendly. You'd be passing on *bad* luck. So what they do is pass it on to a charity. Give it to a priest or something. So maybe that's how Scampion came to be in possession of the ticket. Someone gave it him knowing that he couldn't present it himself, so he wouldn't be incurring bad luck. Knowing, too, that he would pass it on for them to some charitable cause.'

'A priest, perhaps?'

'Yes.'

'You could be right,' said Seymour. 'His sister told me that she was thinking of passing on his clothes to a priest. A particular priest who was a friend of his.'

'I know him. Father Pepe. They got pally over a puncture. Father Pepe had a puncture one day. Scampion was riding by, and he had a repair kit. They got down to it together and friendship bloomed. They had an important thing in common, you see. They were both crazy about bicycles.'

'Someone's told me about this Father Pepe. Isn't there some story about him and betting?'

'That's how he got his bicycle. Before he came to Naples he was in a village out in the countryside and he became persuaded that what he needed in order to perform his duties better was a bicycle. The parish, you see – or whatever Catholics call them – was a widespread one and the alternative was to walk on foot. But Father Pepe was a modernist, in his way, and he decided to buy a bicycle.

'Being a lowly priest, he hadn't any money of his own and he applied to his bishop. The bishop was not a modernist and didn't think much of the idea. But Pepe was not the man to give up. He decided to place a bet with the National Lottery, reasoning that God would know better than the bishop and might be willing to favour his purpose. And, blow me, he won.

'Not enough money, though, to buy a bicycle. But Father Pepe wasn't daunted. Arguing that God had pointed the way, he reckoned that all that was necessary was to persevere. So he placed another bet. And, bless me, that one came good, too. After that there was no stopping him and he soon had enough money to buy a bicycle.

'Unfortunately, he didn't stop there. Reasoning again – he was a bit over-given to reasoning, was Father Pepe – that God had not shown him the way for nothing, he placed more bets and won more money, all of which he gave to charity. Until the lottery office complained and the bishop stopped him.'

'I think I've heard part of this story before.'

'You may well have. Father Pepe is now famous throughout Naples. He has fulfilled every Neopolitan's dream – he has devised a system for winning the lottery. And then the Church made him stop, and swore him to secrecy, and took away all his money. As, in their experience, the Church always does.'

Neither Seymour nor Chantale was a great one for taking a siesta but that day it was so hot that after lunch they went back to the *pensione*. There was a tiny patio at the back and Chantale took a book out there. There was no wind on the patio – there was no wind anywhere in Naples, except, possibly, up on the heights overlooking the bay – but the

70

high walls surrounding the garden made it shady and therefore cool.

She hadn't been reading long when she became aware that she had been joined. A small boy crossed the patio on hands and knees, crawled to the edge and paused beside a tub containing an orange tree. There was a step down into the small garden, a big step for a tiny boy on all-fours, and he paused for a moment to consider it, his back against the tub.

'Fall,' he said.

He spoke in Arabic and Chantale replied, without thinking, in Arabic, too.

'Would you like me to lift you down?' she asked.

The little boy regarded her unthinkingly for a moment and then said: 'Backwards.'

He swivelled himself round, and lowered his rear end over the steps.

Chantale watched him in case of accidents.

'Always go down steps backwards,' he told her.

'A good idea!' agreed Chantale.

The little girl she had met earlier came out on to the patio, scooped up the small boy, and was going to take him inside, but he protested vigorously. She stopped uncertainly, then made up her mind.

'He does not disturb you, Signora?' she said politely to Chantale.

'Not at all,' replied Chantale.

'Where do you want to be?' she asked the small boy. 'Up there or down here?'

'Down here,' said the small boy.

She put him down, but then at once he climbed back up the steps and sat again with his back to the tub. The girl sighed.

'Does the Signora have a brother?' she asked.

'No,' said Chantale, 'but I know they can be trying sometimes.'

'Atiya!' called a voice from inside.

The little girl disappeared.

A moment later the mother came out.

71

'He is not being a nuisance?' she said anxiously. She spoke in Italian. Chantale's Italian was good enough for her to understand the question but not much more, and she replied in Arabic.

'No, no, not at all!' she said.

'If he is, give me a shout,' said the Arab woman. 'I am just in the kitchen, helping Maria.'

She turned to go but then stopped.

'You do not have any children yourself yet?' she said.

'No.'

'Of course!' said the woman. 'I was forgetting. You are still to marry. I find the customs strange here. That you should be with your plighted man on your own. It is not the way they do it in Libya.'

'Nor in Tangier,' said Chantale laughing.

'It is better, I think,' said the woman. 'This way you get to know each other away from the family.'

'That is true,' said Chantale. 'But sometimes the family is a great support.'

'That also is true,' said the woman. 'It is true in my case. Without my husband's family I do not know what I should have done.'

'But sometimes the family can be overwhelming,' said Chantale. 'Especially if it is not entirely your own family.'

'That is true,' said the woman seriously. 'My husband found it so, certainly. Of course, he did not know my family for long. Sometimes I think that that made it easier. He was good with them, but . . . It was difficult and would have become more difficult. It is easier for women to adjust, I think. Because we have our children. So perhaps it was better the way it fell out. That it should be me, not him, that was left. Even though it is hard.'

'It is always hard, I think,' said Chantale, 'in a foreign country. Sometimes better but always hard.'

'One's hope is that it will be less hard for them,' said the woman, gesturing towards her children.

'You mean to stay?' asked Chantale.

'What choice do I have?' said the woman.

72

She made as if to go but then stopped again. Chantale guessed that it was a relief for her to be able to talk about her situation in her own language and with a fellow Arab.

'But sometimes I feel bitter,' she said. 'The people here are nice. They have been good to me. But why did they come to my country in the first pace, bringing their killing? But, then, if they had not, I would not have met Tonio. And the little ones wouldn't have been here.'

She gestured again to the children. Chantale could see that they determined everything for her in a way that she could not herself imagine, having no children of her own. Yet? That was hard to imagine, too. Chantale had always had to fight fiercely but she had fought for herself, to make her own way in a man's world. Whichever way you defined it, whether it had been the Arab world of her Moroccan mother or the army world of her French father, it had been a man's world. The French had been good to her. They had opened doors. It was through them that she had learned about this other, this European world in which women seemed to be beginning to play a part. She had sensed that in the end it was the world for her, it had to be, and she had fought hard to belong to it.

But for her mother it must have been different. She had had her own world and after her husband had died she must have been tempted to revert to it. But, like this woman now, she had had something else to fight for beside herself: her child. And that, Chantale suddenly realized, now, made all the difference.

Seymour had been told that Father Pepe could be found most afternoons working in the grounds of a poor church on the outskirts of Naples. Father Pepe was used to poor churches. He had had the care of one himself before the bishop has translated him to the city, where he could keep an eye on him. What he was not used to, however, was the absence of greenery. There had not initially been much greenery at his previous church, which had been up in the mountains, mostly on bare rock; but over the years he had succeeded in changing that by loving cultivation. Now, in his new church in Naples, he found himself on equally stony soil and had had to start all over again.

In some respects, though, his situation was better. There might not be any grass, not many trees, but what astonished him was that there were flowers in abundance. Every balcony – and almost every house had a balcony, they rose one above another in even the shabbiest of streets – was like a miniature garden. Bright red geraniums thrust their heads out of window boxes, pots of carnations bloomed at every corner. Vines softened the glare of the sun against the white stucco of the walls. If they could do it, reasoned Father Pepe, why couldn't he?

And so soon vines began to creep up the dilapidated walls of the church, the brown, scorched dust which surrounded it became green, and the church was now approached through borders of brightly coloured flowers.

All this required labour, which, the bishop was relieved to see, now occupied most of Father Pepe's free hours, and water. Water, actually, was Father Pepe's chief problem for the church was on a slight promontory and any water had to be carried up from a pump in the square below.

There were mutters about this; for was it right that good water should be used in this frivolous way when it might better be spent on softening the lives of those nearer at hand?

Father Pepe had, however, checked on this. There was plenty of water. The pump was fed from a spring which, in the experience of even the oldest square-dweller, had never dried up. And were not the flowers in their own way a tribute to God?

Faced with such tricky theological speculation, the critics backed off. Some bold spirits ventured to say that they liked it. The spirit of the balconies rose in support of Father Pepe and to everyone's surprise the congregation began to increase. The bishop began to keep an even more anxious eye on what was going on.

So there was no shortage of people ready to tell Seymour where the church and Father Pepe might be found.

'You go to the Gradini di Chiaia,' they said, confident that even the strangest of strangers would know where that was. Seymour, going by the name, was thrown for the moment, for *chiaia* meant quay and the street was nowhere near the sea. He soon learned, however, that the street was famous throughout Naples for its flowers. It descended in steps and on every step there were baskets of flowers. Working, as the Neapolitans appeared to do, by association, one bunch of flowers led to another, and they directed Seymour accordingly. Despite this he found the church.

He knew it was the right church when he saw the bicycle. It leaned against the wall of the church. Its owner was at first nowhere to be found but then the small elderly figure of the priest came into view carrying two huge wooden buckets by a yoke over his shoulders. When he saw Seymour he put the buckets down with relief.

'If only you could carry them on the bicycle!' said Seymour.

'I've tried it,' said Father Pepe, 'but it won't work. You can only carry one bucket at a time in the basket and by the time you've pushed bicycle and bucket up the hill twice, it's not worth it.'

He sat down on a stone and mopped his brow with the sleeve of his habit.

'Were you wanting to see me about something?' he asked.

'I wanted to talk to you about someone,' said Seymour.

'Oh, yes?'

'An Englishman. Whom I think you knew. His name was Scampion.'

'I knew Signor Scampion,' said the priest quietly.

'You had, of course, interests in common,' said Seymour, glancing at the bicycle.

'Many interests in common,' agreed the priest.

'My interest,' said Seymour, 'is in how he came to die. I am an English police officer.'

75

'He was stabbed,' said Father Pepe. 'In the street.'

'I know.'

'Many people are stabbed in Naples. Life is cheap in poor streets.'

'I understand that,' said Seymour. 'But I don't think this was quite like that. He was not the man to get involved in brawls. And his money was not taken.'

'Sometimes an innocent man standing by –' began Father Pepe.

Seymour shook his head.

'Scampion was not standing by,' he said. 'He was killed deliberately. And for a purpose.'

He took out the betting slip and gave it to Father Pepe.

'I wondered if this could be something to do with the purpose,' he said.

Father Pepe looked at the slip. 'It is, of course, an ordinary ticket for the National Lottery.'

'Did Scampion buy tickets in the lottery? This was found in his pocket.'

The priest looked puzzled.

'I did not know he betted,' he said. 'It surprises me. I was under the impression that he didn't. We talked about betting once. I was explaining to him how I came to own a bicycle – I used the money I won by betting,' he said apologetically. 'Signor Scampion said that was all right. I was putting the money to good use. He had no objection to betting from that point of view, he said. Although he thought that poor people shouldn't bet. They would only lose their money.

'He said that was the reason why he never betted himself. He knew he would never win anything. I said it wasn't quite like that. I tried to explain about odds.'

He shook his head, smiling. 'But Signor Scampion was no mathematician. He just laughed and said he had learned he was not a lucky person. He never won raffles or things like that. I said to him that there was no such thing as a lucky person. It was just a matter of odds. The personal qualities of people did not come into it. I am a mathematician, you see,' he explained. 'I studied mathematics before I became a priest. And I believe it is just a matter of arithmetic. But I couldn't persuade him. He insisted it was luck and some people had luck and others didn't. I said, that's what they all believe. But it's just superstition. Ignorant superstition.'

'And yet he had the ticket in his pocket,' said Seymour. 'That is what puzzles me.'

'Someone suggested to me that he might have been given it. And that he might have intended to pass it on.'

'It is possible.'

'They suggested that he might possibly have been going to pass it on to you.'

'Me?'

'Because you were a friend who might be able to put it to better use.'

Father Pepe shook his head.

'I – I don't have anything to do with betting now,' he said.

'This, of course, would have been for charity.'

'Even for charity,' said the priest quickly. 'I try to have nothing to do with it nowadays.'

He looked at the lottery ticket again.

'Is there anything special about it? Anything unusual?'

Father Pepe gazed at the ticket.

'It looks as if the number has come straight from the Smorfia,' he said. 'In which case it might give you a clue to the identity of the person who bought it.'

'A person, anyway,' agreed Seymour. 'The address is that of the Foundling Hospital. And part of the number is the number of a person who was admitted to it.'

'The personal number, yes,' said Father Pepe. 'Then I can see why it might have been special to them and why they might have wished to use it in the lottery. But why would the ticket have been given away?'

'Perhaps because the date had passed?' suggested Seymour.

'And why was it in Signor Scampion's pocket?' said Father Pepe, thinking.

Suddenly his brow cleared.

'Could it be,' he said, 'that the ticket was passed on, or thrown away, precisely because it was out of date? The time limit had expired. It no longer mattered. But somehow it came into the possession of Signor Scampion for whom it *did* matter. Not because of the possibility of winning the lottery but because of the person. He kept the ticket because it spoke to him of the person.'

Chapter Six

When Seymour came out of the *pensione* the next morning he found Giuseppi talking to a young man in the street.

'You can't do this, Bruno!' he was saying.

'She needs it!' said the young man. 'The money's not come through yet.'

'I spoke to them yesterday. I went down to the office with her. And Rinaldo and Pietro, too. And they promised they would do something about it.'

'Yes, but when?' said the young man. 'When? And meanwhile she's got to live.'

'The family will look after her.'

'The family *is* looking after her, I know. But, Giuseppi, your brother is a sick man. Not much money goes into that house. And there are others to be thought of, too. It's too much!'

He put his hand on Giuseppi's arm.

'Don't get me wrong,' he said. 'I know the family's doing what it can. And I know you do your bit, too, Giuseppi. But, hell, you've got others to think of as well. With your son living out there, too, and you having to look after Julia and Francesca. All I'm saying is I want to do my bit, too. I'm in a job. The money comes in regularly. Tonio was a mate of mine, right? I promised him I would help if need be. All I'm doing is keeping that promise.'

'Yes, but Bruno, you have other people to think of too. Your mother.'

'She's no expense. We've got the house and she eats

79

like a bird. It costs nothing. Look, I'm only giving what I can spare.'

'You're very generous, Bruno, but –'

'Come on, take it! Take it!' said the young man, pushing a bundle of notes into Giuseppi's hands.

'Why do I have to give it her?' asked Giuseppi. 'Why can't you give it her?'

'It would look better coming from you. You're Tonio's uncle. If it came from me, people would talk. They would say, hey, what's going on? Why is he giving her money?'

'Well, you've answered that, haven't you? Because you were Tonio's mate.'

'Yes, but you know what people are. They would say: what's the money for? What is she giving him in exchange? And I couldn't bear that, I couldn't bear them thinking . . . It would hurt me, Giuseppi. I would think I had not protected her name. Her name! The widow of my mate! Christ, what would Tonio think! What would he say if he came back? In a dream, perhaps, if he came back to me in a dream – Christ! My mate! His name as well as hers! Jesus!'

'Now, now, Bruno, it's all right!' said Maria, coming out of the *pensione* and putting her arms around him. 'Everyone knows you've been a true friend to Tonio, and we thank you for that.'

'It's the things people say, Maria! About her being black and all that. They ask where did he pick her up? What was she doing for a living? Was she a – oh, Maria, you can't believe what people say!'

'And you shouldn't believe what they say!' said Giuseppi sharply. 'Do they think a decent boy like Tonio would pick for a wife a woman of that sort?'

'And anyone who's talked to her for five minutes,' said Maria angrily, 'should know that she's not like that!'

'But they talk, Maria, they talk! They say: what is she doing here?'

'Look, she's here because she married Tonio. And that makes her as much of a Neapolitan as Francesca is –'

'She certainly is!' said Francesca, coming out of the *pensione*.

'Francesca! You keep out of it!'

'Let them talk, Bruno!' said Francesca fiercely. 'There's plenty I could say about *them*!'

'You're not saying anything, Francesca. Get back inside!'

'She's pure, Maria, and loyal. Loyal to Tonio. Despite what people say.'

'Of course she is!' said Giuseppi indignantly.

'Sometimes I could stick a knife in them! When they say things about her.'

'It's just idle talk –'

'They say they've seen her!'

'Well, that's absolute rubbish!'

'No, no, it's true. I've seen her myself. But it's not as they suppose. She's an innocent and doesn't know our ways, that's all. And sometimes people lead her on. I tried to warn her. But she just gave me a stubborn look, as if to say it was none of my business. But it *is* my business, Maria, now that Tonio's gone. Her honour is in my hands. So when I saw her, I tried to tell her.'

He shrugged. 'But maybe there was no need. The way things turned out. But anyway it wasn't her fault. She doesn't know her way around and people take advantage of her. It makes me so angry, Maria, it makes me so angry!'

'And rightly so,' said Maria soothingly. 'But, look, Bruno, perhaps you're right. We shouldn't make things worse by doing things which might give rise to such talk. I'll tell you what: give *me* the money, and *I'll* give it her.'

'Would you, Maria?' said Bruno gratefully. 'Oh, thank you.'

'Mind you,' said Maria, 'one day I'm going to let her know who the money came from.'

'There's no need –' began Bruno.

'Oh, but there is, Bruno. There is.'

She gave him a kiss.

'You're a good boy, Bruno,' she said. 'A good son to your mother, and a true friend to Tonio.'

* * *

'The things I do for love!' said the Marchesa glumly.

She was sitting on a pile of rags in front of the Palazzo Reale. Behind her stretched the long façade of the Palazzo with its multiplicity of statues: of Roger of Sicily, Frederick the Second of Hohenstaufen, Charles the First of Anjou, Alonzo the First of Aragon, Charles the Fifth, the Emperor. Charles the Third of Bourbon, Napoleon's general and Naples's king. Murat, and so on. The sun glared off the façade and bounced up off the dust of the Piazza del Plebiscito and anyone out in the middle, as the Marchesa pointed out bitterly, caught the full effect. 'I shall melt away entirely,' she declared. 'Into a puddle. And then the dogs will come and lick me up.'

'You have some way to go yet,' said Seymour, taking a positive view.

She patted the rags beside her.

'Come and sit beside me,' she said, 'and melt, too.'

'I am waiting for my fiancée,' said Seymour.

'Come and wait here,' directed the Marchesa. 'Then she will see you and become all jealous.'

'Well . . .'

'It is good for a woman to become jealous,' insisted the Marchesa. 'And men, too, of course. That is one of the things we Italians know. It is good for a person's love life. I make people jealous all the time. It is my contribution to the general well-being of the planet.'

'You know, I don't think I will sit there with you.'

She pouted.

'Oh, well, be like that,' she said. 'Although it is true that two people sitting on this disgusting heap would make one even hotter.'

'Whose love are you doing it for?'

'Vincente's. My cousin.'

'You're waiting for him?'

'I'm waiting for him to come and take these filthy things away.'

'What does he want with a bundle of rags?' said Seymour, mystified.

'They're not rags. They're skins. Goatskins. Water-bags,' she explained. 'For the racers. Vincente's had to organize it all now that Scampion has gone to teach the angels how to bicycle. I'm just minding them while he finds the man who will handle the distribution on Saturday. And the sooner he does that, the better. Before I disappear entirely.'

Chantale came into view at that point and was immediately hailed by the Marchesa.

'Hello, my dear! I've been looking after your fiancé for you.'

'How kind of you!'

'He has remained faithful. So far. But perhaps it is as well you came when you did.'

She patted the goatskins. 'Come and sit beside me. I am establishing an oasis.'

'Wouldn't you do better to do it under a tree?'

'Undoubtedly. But this was where Vincente left the skins. Right out in the sun!'

'Couldn't you keep an eye on them from the shade? There's an arcade over there.'

'Where the letter-writers are? Well, yes, I could, couldn't I? And rush out and squawk if anyone does anything untoward to them. Although I fear no one will. Unless a dog pees on them,' said the Marchesa hopefully.

She rose up off the pile and dusted herself down.

'Ugh! The smell!' she said. 'I shall never get rid of it. Perhaps I ought to go back to the hotel and change my clothes.'

'Oh, don't do that!' said Seymour hastily, fearing that he and Chantale were going to be required to take over the guardianship of the skins. 'At least, not until Vincente comes.'

'Why, he's coming now,' said the Marchesa. 'I can see him over there. What a relief!'

Vincente was coming towards them, accompanied by a man in a dark suit and two men pushing a hand-cart.

'At last!' said the Marchesa.

'I came as quickly as I could,' said Vincente defensively.

'I felt I had been left to die in the desert,' said the Marchesa. 'Not the least of the army's atrocities!'

'Luisa, you mustn't say things like that! Not where people can hear you.'

'A human sacrifice!' said the Marchesa loudly. 'Burnt at the stake. For the greater satisfaction of the Church and the people.'

'Don't make such a fuss, Luisa!'

'Some dogs came,' said the Marchesa 'and did an unmentionable thing. On the goatskins.'

'Oh, God!' cried Vincente. 'Where? Where?'

The Marchesa laughed.

'Let's go and have an ice-cream,' she said to Seymour and Chantale. 'Under the arches, perhaps? As you suggested?'

There were some tables beneath the arches, where they could eat their ice-creams in the shade, and from them they could see along the arcade to where the public letter-writers were busy at their desks.

'It's like it is in Tangier,' said Chantale, interested.

'It's not like it is in Milan,' said the Marchesa. 'The south is impossibly backward.'

In front of each desk there was often a little queue of clients waiting patiently. People who needed a letter-writer's services were, of course, illiterate and usually poor. Many of them, judging by their clothes, had come in recently from the countryside and were probably writing back to their families. There were some men but most of them were women, elderly ladies dressed in black. But some were young, often barely more than girls, sent in to the city to earn their living as servants and relieve the burden on their families.

In one of the queues was the Arab woman, Jalila. Seymour was surprised because from the way she had spoken he had assumed that she could write. Perhaps she could, but in Arabic, and was wanting to send a letter to an Italian, and was not yet confident enough of her ability in the language to do so unaided.

'Have you been to the Teatro?' asked the Marchesa.
   'The Teatro?'
'The Teatro San Carlo,' said the Marchesa, indicating a long building next to the Palazzo. 'It's one of the largest opera houses in the world. As big, they claim, as the one in Milan. Of course, it's closed now – they're between seasons – but they'll let you put your head in if you ask, and it's worth a look. It *would* be closed,' said the Marchesa disgustedly, 'when I got here.'

'Here I sit,' said the Marchesa gloomily, 'while the world goes on without me.'
   She had hardly tasted her ice-cream and was deep in thought looking across the piazza to where Vincente was supervising the transfer of the skins on to the hand-cart.
   'I blame bicycling,' she said suddenly.
   'Certainly, bicycling has much to answer for,' said Seymour, 'but –'
   'I wouldn't be here,' said the Marchesa, 'if it were not for blasted bicycles.'
   'That's a bit hard, on bicycles,' said Seymour.
   'No, it's not. If it had not been for that stupid quarrel –'
   'What quarrel was this?'
   'The one between Dion and Gifford.' And then, seeing his blankness: 'Does this mean nothing to you?'
   'Nothing. Except . . .' Faint bells began to tinkle. 'Is this not something to do with bicycling?'
   'There you are! Bicycling. As I said.'
   'It does not mean a great deal to me, I'm afraid, Marchesa.'
   'I should think not. It shouldn't mean anything to anyone. But it appeared to mean a great deal to the idiots in Florence who expelled D'Annunzio. And, consequently, me.'

85

'This has, unfortunately, escaped me.'

'Lucky you. And lucky England, which remains blissfully ignorant of anything that is happening in the world outside its shores. One of these days there is going to be a great war. And England will be the last to hear of it.'

'Enlighten my ignorance, and I will see what I can do for the rest of my country.'

'The Prime Minister was there. The Prime Minister of Italy, that was. And some of Count Dion's supporters went up to him and assaulted him. Insulted him, too, which to Italians is even worse. And then Gifford's supporters took umbrage and assaulted *them*. And Gabrieli was in the thick of things –'

'Gabrieli?'

'D'Annunzio. Well, he would be. If there was limelight going, he was never one to shrink from thrusting himself into it. But this time he had gone too far. This was the Prime Minister, and politicians, for some reason, take that seriously. So D'Annunzio had to go. Out of Italy, I mean. And Alessandro, my husband, had a business interest in the matter and was incensed, and then, for some reason which I do not fully understand, he blamed me and I had to go, too.'

'And for some reason, which I, too, do not fully understand, you blame bicycling?'

'Yes.'

'I'm sorry, I don't quite see the connection –'

'*Dion, Gifford.*'

'Oh, wait a minute. The two cycling magazines, *Vélo* and *Auto-Vélo*. One yellow, one green?'

'*That*'s right. Gifford started the green magazine and then they quarrelled and de Dion started the yellow one.'

'And for some reason de Dion's supporters assaulted the Prime Minister?'

'That's right.'

'Over bicycling!'

'Well, not just over bicycling. This was the time when France was divided over the Dreyfuss case – you know, that poor, daft French officer who was found guilty, quite wrongly, of spying for the Germans. Half the nation said he was guilty, the other half said he was innocent. He was a Jew, you see, and people took sides accordingly. On one side Dreyfuss's supporters, socialist, republican, anti-Church; on the other, the traditional supporters of the army, conservative, *very* Catholic, imperialist. And anti-Jewish, of course. Count Dion was very much one of the latter. Gifford was one of the former. It gave an extra edge to their bicycling debates.

'Now, the Prime Minister, although not exactly socialist, was certainly not a member of the latter group. He had, in fact, done quite a lot for the army – started the war with Libya, for example – but that wasn't enough for them. So they attacked him. That incensed him, and also his supporters, who happened to be in the majority, and it was decided that an example had to be made. It couldn't be de Dion, because he was so powerful and so rich and was supporting the army with arms: and so it had to be D'Annunzio.

'Alessandro was very angry. The Prime Minister, say what you like, had at least started the war against Libya, and things were going swimmingly, and Alessandro was making lots of money: and then these idiots came along and threatened to wreck everything! And all, as he saw it, because of a dispute over bicycling! Someone had to suffer: and, unfortunately, it turned out to be me.'

Jalila went past.

'That's the trouble,' said Marchesa. 'We go over there and then they come over here.'

Vincente had finished supervising the loading of the skins and now came across to them.

'Show them the opera house,' directed the Marchesa.

Vincente obediently took them to the side door.

'The main entrance won't be open,' he said. 'The Teatro is between seasons.'

He seemed to have no difficulty in gaining entrance for them. They stood for a while and admired the sweep of boxes, the gilt dripping from the ceiling, the faded plushness of the seats. Seymour tried to imagine what it would be like with an orchestra in the pit and performance on stage.

Chantale did, too. She had never been to the opera.

'I don't think they have an opera house in Tangier,' she said. 'And if they did, and a woman went to it, it would cause a riot.'

'Really?' said Vincente, astonished.

'Yes. We have theatres, of course. But only men can go to them.'

'Incredible!' said Vincente. 'Why, half the point of going to the opera is to study the women.'

'I think that's what they object to,' said Chantale drily.

When they came out of the opera house, the Marchesa was nowhere to be seen.

'She's doing it *again*!' said Vincente crossly. 'She makes an appointment and then disappears! She insisted I came with her this morning and now she's wandered off!'

But then the Marchesa came into view at the other end of the arcade.

'Where have you been?' scolded Vincente.

'To church,' said the Marchesa.

'I don't believe you!' said Vincente.

'Well, I have.'

'You *never* go to church.'

'I do sometimes. I'm a good Catholic. Quite.'

'Well, I don't believe you've just been to one.'

'Well, I have.'

'Which one?' said Vincente sceptically.

'The San Rocco. It's just along there. Behind the Palazzo. I heard children singing so I went in. You often hear them in the San Rocco.'

'How do you know that?' said Vincente, still sceptical.

'Because I often go to hear them.'

'Really?'

'And sometimes I go to other churches as well. The San Lorenzo, for instance.'

'Luisa, you're making this up. I don't believe there *is* a San Lorenzo.'

'Yes, there is. It's where Boccaccio first saw Fiammetta. You have probably never heard of Fiammetta, Vincente. She was the great love of Boccaccio's life. Come to think of it, Vincente, you are such an oaf that you have probably never heard of Boccaccio, either.'

'I *have* heard of Boccaccio,' said Vincente sulkily.

'Well, that's where he first met her. And the thing is, Vincente, that when he first met her, there was music. "There was a singing compact of sweetest melody." That's what he says. And it struck me, Vincente, because I think that's how it should be. At supreme moments in one's life, one needs music. I have always believed that. When one falls in love, it must be to music. Why didn't I remember that when I met Alessandro? There was no music when he was around. Only the crisp rustle of banknotes.'

They parted from the Marchesa and Vincente at the end of the arcade and had not noticed Miss Scampion until she emerged from the shadows of one of the arches.

'I did not wish to be seen,' said Miss Scampion. 'I did not wish to have to acknowledge . . . that woman. She is not a respectable woman.'

'The Marchesa?'

'So called. I don't think she is entitled to call herself that now. The title came from her previous husband. The present husband has no title. He is, I believe, a financier. I have nothing against people who work in finance. Some of my best friends are in the City. My own cousin, Jeremy, is what I believe is called a jobber. Although I gather that sometimes the word has unfortunate connotations in other walks of life. And he is a very respectable man. Occasionally he does things for the Church. Advises them, you know, on financial matters. And, certainly, they sometimes seem badly in need of financial advice. I have met some of his friends and they are *most* respectable. But that is not always the case in finance and certainly not, or so I gather, in Rome. I have heard some doubtful things about her husband. Rich, oh yes: but where do his riches come from? From dealing with unsavoury people. He certainly does not have a title. And so, certainly, now, no more does she.'

'You are harsh, Miss Scampion.'

'Not without reason, Mr Seymour. I saw what that woman did to my brother.'

'And what did she do?'

She was silent for a moment. Then she said:

'She led him on. As she led everybody on. Into wildnesses and excesses of all kinds.' She wrinkled her nose as at a bad smell. 'Some of them,' she said, lowering her voice, 'sexual. Although that was not, of course, the case with Lionel. She was most improper; and she encouraged other people to be improper, too. Those nice boys –'

She stopped.

'Nice boys, Miss Scampion?'

'Lionel's friends. They had formed themselves into a club, to meet and talk. About politics, you know, and masculine things like that: Lionel used to attend some of their meetings, and I was always very pleased because I felt he needed male company, which I could not supply. It took him into a wider world. And gave him an opportunity to associate with people from good families.

'Because they all came from good families, you know. As you would expect, since they were almost all officers. I was so pleased when Lionel told me about them. I had felt, you see, when we were in London, and in Budapest, that his friends were not always altogether suitable. Not always, to my mind, masculine enough. So I was very pleased when he told me about these new friends he had been making. The army gives a certain stiffening, you know.

'And these boys were so nice, so young and fresh. So idealistic. They wanted good things for their country. That's what they used to talk about, you know. What Italy needed, what way it should go. They were so *patriotic* – which, sadly, you don't always find in the young these days.

'And well behaved. Perfect manners, they all had perfect manners. Which, again, you don't always find in young men these days.

'And religious, too. Catholic, of course. Well, you would expect that in Italy. I was a little worried at first that Lionel might – well, he was always such a one for enthusiasms – might be drawn in that direction. Fortunately he held firm! Our family has always been good C. of E. Except on the Scottish side, where we are people of the manse. But I thought it was a good sign that they were religious. It showed that they were thinking people, people of a certain depth.'

She laughed. 'And they did take that side seriously, you know. They even gave themselves a religious name, the Club, that is.'

'Sursum Corda?' suggested Seymour.

'Why, yes!' said Miss Scampion, surprised. 'How did you know?'

'Someone mentioned the name to me.'

'Of course, it is well known, I gather. Although I had not come across it myself until we arrived in Florence. And suddenly *everyone* seemed to be talking about it. Among Lionel's friends, at least. And they seemed such a nice, respectable group for him to have fallen in with.

'But then That Woman came along!'

'The Marchesa?'

'So-called. Yes. And she led them astray. She was the Serpent, Mr Seymour: the Serpent in Eden, for so Florence seemed to me. A veritable Paradise. And she spoiled it.'

'How – how exactly did she spoil it, Miss Scampion?'

'She turned their heads. As soon as she appeared, they all clustered round her. And made themselves silly. She was like a bright butterfly and they all tried to catch her. But what was worse, Mr Seymour, was that it wasn't just their eyes that men turned, it was their minds. She diverted

them away from all those noble things they had been dis-
cussing and directed them into Frivolous Pursuits!'

'Frivolous Pursuits?'

'Dancing, partying, wildnesses of all kinds!'

'Good heavens!'

'Yes,' said Miss Scampion, pleased with the effect she
had produced. 'You understand so well!'

'And Lionel . . .?'

'Lost his head, too, I am afraid.'

Miss Scampion walked on beside them, pushing her
bicycle.

'Can I assist you, Miss Scampion? The street is rather
crowded at this point.'

'Thank you – it *is* a little unwieldy. At close quarters, that
is. Do you ride, Miss de Lissac?'

'Well, no, I'm afraid.'

'You're used to horses, I expect. Military families are
good with horses. They have to be. The men, I mean. But
often the women are, too. They grow up with horses. I had
rather hoped, when I was a girl and we used to go and stay
with my uncle – the army one, you know – that he would
keep ponies. But he said that they ate you out of house and
home. And drink, too, which was much more important.
So I never really rode myself.

'I did once, just before we moved to Florence, suggest to
Lionel that he bought a horse. It would look so dashing,
you know. I really feel he would have looked well on
horseback. Better than on a bicycle. More, sort of, impos-
ing! But he took the same view as Uncle and said that we
couldn't afford it. And instead, when we got to Florence,
he went for a bicycle.

'I was cross at first. But afterwards I was so glad! For if
he had done what I suggested, and gone for a horse, it
would have been disastrous!'

'Disastrous, Miss Scampion?'

'Yes. Because, you see, That Woman rode a horse. Every
Saturday morning. I am sure she did it deliberately,
because that was when the men did their practising on

their bicycles, and she wished to lure them away. But she did not succeed. They stayed true to their bicycles.

'Except – and this was unfortunate – for D'Annunzio. She succeeded in luring him. Well, of course, that was quite understandable for he was a keen equestrian. But I felt it was unfortunate, for he had such an influence on others. And particularly on those fine young men. They hung upon his words. He fired them – fired them with enthusiasm for Italy and for all those great ideals they discussed at their meetings. When Lionel came home and told me what D'Annunzio had been saying I couldn't help weeping with emotion.

'So it could have been disastrous when that evil woman succeeded in luring him away and they went riding together. They all – all those fine young men, Lionel, too – might have followed him. But they stayed true – true to their bicycles.

'And that, I think, was Lionel's saving.'

Chapter Seven

Every day Seymour had made a point of dropping in at the small restaurant behind the Porta del Carmine and by now he had become quite well known there. The owner did not even wait to be told but placed a bowl of snail soup before him at the table. Seymour had been tempted by the fish soup, the Zuppa alla Marinar, which he had seen at other street restaurants, but the owner did not serve any.

'Snails,' he said, 'are my business.'

'And quite right, too!' said Seymour's previous acquaintance, the Smorfia-reading carpenter, looking up from his bowl. 'Your snails, Ernesto, are exquisite.'

'I do my best,' said the restaurant owner modestly.

He did not, in fact, own very much, just the big pot of oil simmering on the fire he had built in the street, the table and chairs, which he had probably borrowed, and, of course, his raw materials, contained in a tank-like box.

'Where they can keep fresh,' he explained. 'That's the thing about my snails. They're freshly gathered every day – I'm up on the slopes first thing in the morning – and if they're kept like this they stay fresh.'

'And it shows!' said the carpenter.

Various other bystanders nodded in agreement.

The vendor of snails did not even bring his own water. He relied on an *acquaiolo* further up the street, who was quite prepared to explain the virtues of his own product.

'All the water,' he said, 'comes from the spring at Santa Lucia. I go there every day to get it. One day, perhaps, I will lay a pipe to my stall –'

'Dream on, Alberto!' said the carpenter.

'You scoff,' said the *acquaiolo*, 'but the day approaches.'

'But will it taste the same?' asked the snail-shop owner anxiously. 'When it's been through the pipe?'

'That remains to be seen,' acknowledged the *acquaiolo*.

'I would have to taste it first,' said the restaurant owner, 'before I used it for my snails.'

'And so you shall,' promised the *acquaiolo*. 'And if it is not as good, I will bring you the water myself as I do at present.'

'Thank you, Alberto. It makes all the difference, you see. The water has a sulphur taste, which brings out the best in the snails.'

'I think the water has been changing,' said the carpenter.

'Oh, no!'

'Just a little,' insisted the carpenter, who was evidently something of a connoisseur.

'You really think so?' said the restaurant owner, worried.

'Just a little. A very little.'

'It's all the water that's being drawn off,' said Ernesto. 'It means the water has to come from deeper.'

'That could be it!' said the carpenter.

'Of course, you could argue that it makes it fresher,' said the *acquaiolo*.

'Anyway,' said Seymour, 'the product speaks for itself.'

'That's specialization for you,' said the carpenter. 'And that's why I say Ernesto should stick to his snails.'

'Until I win the lottery!' said Ernesto, smiling.

'Until he wins the lottery!' said the carpenter, sighing. 'That will be a while yet!'

'How have you been doing lately?' asked Seymour.

'Badly! I do all the right things and I've had some good numbers. But somehow they don't come to anything.'

'Me, too!' said Seymour.

'You tried that number we worked out?'

'I did.'

'And . . .?'

'It was close. It was close. But not close enough. I was two numbers out.'

'That *is* close!' said the *acquaiolo*. 'Are you sure you did it right? Maybe we made a little mistake. Because that was a good number, and the fact that it was so close . . . Look, let's go through it again. If there was just a little mistake, maybe you could put it right next time.'

He pulled the Smorfia towards him. 'Now, what was it?'

'A man,' said Seymour. 'Here, at the Porta Carmine. Murdered.'

'15, 13 and 27.'

'That's what I tried.'

'Really?' said the carpenter, disappointed and a little surprised.

'You mean that Englishman?' said the *acquaiolo*.

'Yes.'

'That was a good idea! And it didn't win?'

'No.'

'Funny.'

'Maybe it wasn't particular enough,' said Seymour.

'Man, you mean? Maybe you should have specified Englishman.'

'Can I do that?'

'I don't know. Let's have a look. No, I don't think you can. But you could have tried "foreigner".'

'That could be it!' said the *acquaiolo*.

'Well, could it?' asked Seymour. 'It still doesn't seem specific enough to me. Maybe there is something else we should put in?'

'Like what?'

'I don't know,' confessed Seymour. 'I just feel –'

'You should trust your feelings,' said the *acquaiolo*.

'But refine them,' said the carpenter. 'Sort of narrow them down. Go on thinking.'

'I will,' promised Seymour. 'And you, too.'

'I will,' said the carpenter.

He looked at his watch, and then jumped up.

'Christ!' he said. 'I ought to have been back ten minutes ago. My wife will be up here at any moment.'

He rushed away.

'That was a good idea,' said the *acquaiolo*. 'A really good idea. I should have thought of that! I was here when it happened, you know.'

'You were? When the Englishman was killed?'

'Yes. I was right behind him. At least, the other side of the pillar. I was just bringing some water from the spring. I'd got through a lot that day, I don't know why. Oh, yes, I do: some drovers had come up, and they had all wanted a drink. It was very hot that day. Anyway, I was carrying the water, and I stopped for a moment. Behind the Porta. The bags get quite heavy after a while. I had put them down and was just going to pick them up again when I heard a clatter. That was the bicycle falling over. And then the Englishman fell after it. I went to help him up. And then, Christ, I saw the blood. And froze.'

'Blood?'

'Yes. Coming from his neck. So I knew what had happened. And that it was best to keep out of it.'

'You were as close as that?'

'As close as I am to you.'

'But you must have seen –'

'No, I didn't. I must have been looking down at that moment to pick up the bags. I was conscious of someone brushing past me and then he was gone. Up the street, I suppose. Into one of the *bassi*.'

'Christ!' said Seymour.

'Yes,' said the *acquaiolo*.

'And you didn't see . . . the one who had done it?'

'No. Not at all. But I'd seen enough to know I'd better keep out of it. Recognized the handiwork, you might say.'

'Recognized the . . .?'

'Knew it at once.'

The *acquaiolo* looked around cautiously and lowered his voice.

'Them,' he said.

Chantale had strayed into a back street where all the shops were fruit-sellers. They announced that by hanging garlands of fruit leaves and bunches of grapes over their windows. Most of them had counters outside and these, too, were decorated with leaves and fruit, sometimes by whole branches. The owners stood beside their counters calling to pedestrians as they passed. Chantale had no occasion to buy fruit but she amused herself by listening to the fruit-sellers' calls and trying, with her imperfect Italian, to translate them.

'Eat, drink, and wash your face in them.' These were watermelons, which were also 'redder than the fire of Vesuvius'.

'No passengers!' was another favourite cry. 'If you don't believe, bite one!' Eventually she worked out that this meant 'No worms!'

'There's cinnamon inside!' This, for some reason, referred to apricots. 'Gold, not grapes!' was easy. But 'Ladies' thighs!' was more difficult. 'Ladies' thighs! We adore them!' the street sellers called out. It took some time before Chantale realized that they were talking about pears.

Outside one of the shops she saw the Arab woman, Jalila, trying to effect her purchases with a squirming boy in one arm and the other hand holding her little girl. The little girl detached herself and ran up to Chantale. Jalila spun round after her.

'Hello, Atiya!' said Chantale.

'Signora!' said the little girl, and put her hand in Chantale's.

'Do you mind, Signora?' said Jalila anxiously.

'Not at all. I'll hold her while you get on with your shopping.'

'I'm buying some tomatoes for Maria,' said Jalila. 'I shan't be a moment.'

She put the tomatoes in the basket at her feet and picked it up. That seemed still to require an extra hand.

'Atiya can walk along with me,' said Chantale.

Jalila smiled her thanks.

'He is tired,' she said, indicating the boy in her arm, 'and insists on being carried.'

'He ought to walk,' said Atiya sternly.

'But he is very little still,' said Chantale.

They walked along the street together.

'I saw you yesterday,' said Chantale. 'With the letter-writer. Were you sending a letter back to your family?'

She had a half-hearted idea that she might offer her services.

Jalila looked startled.

'No,' she said. 'I can do that myself. It's the letters in Italian that I find difficult.'

'You seem to speak Italian very well,' said Chantale, 'but I know writing is more difficult.'

'Well, yes,' said Jalila seriously, 'because it has to be just so. Especially when you are writing to someone Exalted.'

She was speaking in Arabic and 'Exalted' didn't seem quite right for an Italian context.

'Not that the letter-writer was much good,' she added tartly.

'And has the pension come through yet?'

'Not yet,' said Jalila. 'They promise it for tomorrow. But things are always "tomorrow" here. There is some hope, though, Giuseppi tells me, that this time it will be different.'

'I hope so,' said Chantale.

'I should be all right,' said Jalila, 'provided it comes through soon. Someone has given me some money, which will cover the next day or two.'

'That must be a relief!' said Chantale.

'Yes. I don't know who it's from. Maria wouldn't tell me.' She hesitated. 'But I think I can guess,' she said.

'Oh?'

'Yes.' She hesitated again. 'There's a man. A friend of Tonio's. Not a relative, just a friend. I don't know whether I should take it. If it was from a relative, of course I would take it. That would be family. But a friend – I don't know.'

She shook her head.

'I don't know. Would it be proper?' she appealed.

'If it comes through Maria,' said Chantale, 'it would surely be proper.'

99

'Yes, that's what I thought. But I have been wondering about it since. You see, if it comes from this man, the one I told you of, Tonio's friend, then – well, it is a bit more complicated. They were close, you see, this man and Tonio. Very close. And he feels that with Tonio gone, and with his family being as old, and frail, as they are, he should take on some of their obligations.'

'Well, that is very nice of him.'

'Yes, it is. But how far should it go? How far should I let him?'

She was silent for a moment. Then she said, with a rush: 'He wants to marry me.'

'Well, that is good. If you want to marry *him*.'

'He is very nice.'

'Well, then –'

'And good. He is a good man.'

'In that case –'

'But . . .' said Jalila.

'You don't want to marry him?'

'I am not sure.'

Chantale knew the feeling.

'He says it is proper. In Naples. For a relative, when a man dies, to take on his responsibilities. To marry his widow and provide for her. It is the way that the family takes responsibility for her. And if there isn't a suitable relative, he says, it is not uncommon for the man's best friend to step in.'

She looked at Chantale. 'It is like that among us, too. As you know. The dead man's brother, or cousin if there is no brother, takes over. Of course, sometimes there is a difficulty. He may not want to, or she may not want to. But usually –'

She broke off.

'But I have always felt,' she resumed, after a moment, 'that it is much to ask. And I made up my mind that if it ever came to me, I would not do it. If the brother were unwilling, would it not breed disharmony? And all the more so if it were not a brother but a friend. And, besides –'

100

She stopped again.

'Yes?'

'There is more to it than that. More than marrying just so as to carry on in the old way. At least, there was in my case. When I married I felt I had come to a crossroads. One of the roads was for things to stay as they were. That would be normal in a marriage. But by marrying Tonio I knew that I would not be able to go down that road. He was a foreigner and things could not be the same. And then he said that he would take me to Italy and I knew that if he did that then things would certainly never be the same again.

'And I did not mind. Because he had told me what it would be like. Oh, I knew that all men spin their stories before marriage, and that afterwards it is not quite like that. But this was different, because he would take me away, right away, from the things that I knew. And I wanted to be taken away.'

She looked at Chantale.

'Do you understand that?' she demanded.

'I think I do,' said Chantale.

'It was not that I hated my family. It was more that I was coming to hate the life. I felt trapped, somehow caught. Caught and put in a cage. Before I had even started! I could see no way out. Somehow I felt doomed. And then Tonio came along, and I thought, maybe it doesn't have to be like that. Maybe I could break out of my cage.

'Oh, I know that there are cages in Italy, too. Different kinds of cages. But there seem to be more doors to the cages here. You feel that if you try, you can go out through one.

'Children are a cage. Oh, I know I should not speak like that. But they are. A dear one, and I would not have it other. Particularly now that Tonio has gone and they are all I have to remind me of him. But they *are* a cage, and I feel caught again. It was not quite what I had wanted when I was a girl, dreaming. Perhaps I did not know what I wanted but it was, somehow, to be free, to fly on my own.

'Well, then I married Tonio, and of course, I was happy. Children came and I was happier still. And the world Tonio had spun for me seemed just around the corner, there, waiting for me to seize it.

'And then Tonio was killed. Shot. By my own people. But by then I did not know who were my own people. Were they my people, or Tonio's? And what of the children? Where they children of my people or of Tonio's?

'Marcello was in no doubt. You know Marcello? Well, you know of him. He is Maria's and Giuseppi's son, Francesca's father. And he was a good friend of Tonio. Moreover, he was his cousin, and had duties. And he said: "Tonio would have wished it, Jalila, and so you must do it. You must come to Naples." And I thought, well, perhaps I will never get out of my cage now, but perhaps, this way, my children will. So I agreed.

'There was someone he knew. A captain. He was Tonio's captain, too. And he had a powerful friend in Rome. And through this friend they were able to fix it, to arrange for us to come to Italy, and be received by Tonio's family.

'So now I am here. And I have found that there are other cages. And perhaps another crossroads. For there are several roads I can go down. One of them is with Bruno. That would be safe and secure. I would no longer have to worry about the children. But I also know that if I take that road, I would not be able to go down any other one. I would never be able to fly for myself. And the dream would have gone.'

Seymour came round the corner and greeted them. Jalila thanked Chantale and detached the little girl's hand. They moved away.

'Let's just walk back down this street,' said Chantale. 'Would you like some ladies' thighs?'

'What?' said Seymour, startled.

Chantale linked her arm through his. 'People here adore them.'

* * *

'They always say it's the Camorra,' said Richards dismissively. 'But, in my experience – and I've been here six years – it never is. There was a time when they were all-powerful in Naples but in recent years they've lost ground. Nowadays they stick to minor stuff, protection and that sort of thing. But Naples is a very conservative place and their old reputation lingers on. It's part of the local folklore. Anything out of the ordinary that happens they put down to the Camorra. If there's a big accident, say. But accidents happen all the time in Naples, as in any big city, and that's nothing to do with the Camorra. Or an especially gory murder. But there's seldom any real reason to suppose it's anything to do with the Camorra. It's, as I say, part of the local folklore. Like the Magic Number.'

'Magic Number?'

'The one that will win the lottery. Every time. If you can only find it. Look, old man, I don't want to go on about this, but Naples is not England. It's not even Italy, or, at least, modern Italy, the Italy of the north. It's still locked in the past, more backward, superstitious. And the Camorra is part of the superstition.'

'They speak of it as if it was real.'

'Well, they would, wouldn't they? That's what I mean. Look, I'm not denying that they exist. But they're not the force they were. They may still do the occasional favour for an old acquaintance but mostly these days they stick to collecting protection money.'

'And Scampion had only just come here and had nothing to protect?'

'Unless you count the consulate and, believe me, old chap, we're not quite that desperate!'

Seymour laughed.

'It was just that the man I spoke to seemed so sure,' he said.

'Oh, they're all sure,' said Richards. 'Sure, but wrong. Look, it couldn't have been the Camorra because he hadn't been here long enough for them even to have heard of him. He couldn't have done anything to get across them because since he arrived he hadn't actually done anything at all! Once I saw what he was like, I took good care of that!'

'Maybe, then,' said Seymour, 'it was something he did *before* he got here.'

Richards shook his head.

'Not even that,' he said. 'If it's the Camorra you're thinking of, you've got to rule them out. The Societies stick to their own territory. The Mafia to Sicily, the Camorra to Naples. They never, but *never*, encroach on anyone else's territory. What Scampion did before he got here is no concern of theirs.'

Seymour had lingered in the consulate longer than he had intended and now he was late for collecting Chantale. He had promised to take her out to dinner at a little fish restaurant that Giuseppi had told him about. The restaurant was along the Posillipo promontory, just beyond the boats, and that was where she would be waiting for him. He had just reached the Capuana Gate when someone hailed him.

It was Miss Scampion.

'Oh, Mr Seymour, I am so glad to have caught you. There is something I must tell you.'

'Really, Miss Scampion? I am afraid I am in rather a hurry just at the moment –'

'I have been thinking about it all day.'

Seymour stopped resignedly.

'About what, Miss Scampion?'

'About the betting slip.'

'The one you found in your brother's trousers?'

'That's right. I think, in retrospect, that I may have given you the wrong impression.'

'How so?'

'I think I may have implied, or even said, that my brother had been deceiving me. Or, at any rate, holding something back from me. And when I found the betting slip I immediately feared the worst. But, as you very rightly told me, there could have been a quite innocent

104

explanation. And, thinking it over calmly – I am afraid that when I spoke to you I was far from calm, I was still, under the impact of the discovery, greatly shocked – I feel I may have been doing him an *Injustice*.

'I had been assuming, God forgive me, that the lottery ticket was evidence of his own . . . his own depravity. That he himself was betting. But that need not have been so, need it? Perhaps somebody else was betting, a friend of his, perhaps, and Lionel was very angry with him, and had, perhaps, taken the slip *away* from him, to save him from the consequences of his actions –'

'Well, yes, Miss Scampion, that is certainly possible, I suppose –'

'That would have been very like Lionel. He always had a very keen sense of what was right and wrong. It would have been very like him to have seized the ticket and said: "No, I cannot allow you to do this!"'

'Well, yes, Miss Scampion –'

'And that would account for his anger.'

'His anger?'

'Yes. I – I think I mentioned to you, Mr Seymour, that I had been feeling for some time that something was amiss. Something had been troubling him, something had been making him angry. And that was most unusual, for normally he had such a sunny disposition, he never seemed to lose his temper. But for some time he had been – well, angry is the only word. He was *angry*.

'And I thought, when I found the lottery ticket, God forgive me, that he was angry with himself. But that need not have been so, need it, Mr Seymour? He could have been angry with the other person. Or, rather, at the sin and not the sinner, as they always taught us in church.'

'Well, yes, that could be so, Miss Scampion –'

'It was so unusual. This anger. I kept out of his way. I had learned that, of course, very early on. To keep out of his way when he was in one of his moods. For often when he was angry, it would spill over on to other things – on to me, for example, which I thought most unfair, as well as the thing which had made him angry in the first place. And

105

this was what happened on this occasion. He became very angry, for instance, about the bicycle parts.'

'Bicycle parts?'

'Yes. He was *very* angry about them. They had sent the wrong ones, you see.'

Seymour began to edge away. 'Well, of course, that is always very annoying. Especially if he needed them –'

'No, no, they weren't for him. It was up at the army base. They had sent the wrong ones. And there were, apparently, rather a lot of them. Lionel became very angry about it. Of course, that was just like him. Taking other people's troubles on his own shoulders. Strictly speaking, of course, it was none of his business. He admitted that. But he said that someone ought to do something. And no one else seemed to be going to. The Italians are a bit like that, I'm afraid. They have a saying about how sweet it is to do nothing. But they carry it to extremes. They are so lax! Even in the army, I'm afraid.'

'These parts were for the army, then?'

'Yes. Doubtless they were defective in some way. And no one was bothering! But one *should* bother, shouldn't one? My uncle – the army one, you know – always used to say you should care for public money as it if was your own. And this almost certainly *was* public money, wasn't it? Someone was wasting it in some way and Lionel had spotted it.

'He was quite acute on things like that. I remember once in the schoolroom he hauled me over the coals for the number of rubber bands I had been using. "Waste not, want not!" he said. I was quite taken aback, and I felt it was very unfair, too. He never seemed to listen to the sermon in church and yet he produced this!'

'The Devil can always quote scripture to suit his own purpose,' said Seymour, sententiously.

Miss Scampion went pink.

'I don't think that is quite appropriate, Mr Seymour!' she said severely.

Chapter Eight

Seymour and Chantale were still sitting at breakfast when the Arab woman, Jalila, came into the room, holding a child with each hand. Her face was radiant.

'It's come!' she said. 'It came through this morning.'

She went across to old Giuseppi, caught up his hand and kissed it.

'I owe it to you!' she said.

'Nonsense!' said Giuseppi, patting her awkwardly on the head. 'It is only your desert. As the widow of an Italian soldier.'

'Without you I would have done nothing!' declared Jalila.

'It has really come through?'

'*Si.*'

She took out a letter and brandished it.

'It says here that I will receive fifty on the first of every month. And with it there was a piece of paper I had to take to the post office and then they would give me the money. And I took it,' said Jalila triumphantly, 'and they gave it!'

Maria came out of the kitchen and embraced her.

'It will make all the difference, Jalila,' she said. 'Now you will not have to beg.'

'No one should have to beg,' said Giuseppi. 'Least of all, when it is your due.'

'I am glad of it for the sake of the children,' said Jalila. 'It is bad for children if they see their mother begging.'

She looked at Maria.

'And I am glad for the sake of Tonio, too,' she said. 'He would not have liked to see his wife beg.'

'He would have been angry,' said Giuseppi, 'that his wife should have had to wait so long!'

'And Marcello, too!' She looked at Maria. 'For I am sure he has had a hand in this.'

'Marcello is a good boy!' said Giuseppi.

Francesca came out and put her arms round Jalila.

'I will write to him and tell him,' she said. 'I know he will be pleased.'

'And your brother, too,' Jalila said to Giuseppi. 'He has done what he could for me. But I know it has not been easy.'

'He would have done more if he could.'

'I know.'

Giuseppi blew his nose loudly.

'I have brought some eggs,' said Jalila. 'It is little, I know,' she said apologetically, 'but –'

'You shouldn't have,' said Maria. 'You should have given them to the children.'

'For you!' Jalila insisted.

'For the family. I shall make a cake. For everyone. And the children will help me.'

She took the children by the hand and started to lead them into the kitchen. Then she stopped.

'No,' she said. 'Francesca will make the cake.'

'*Can* Francesca make a cake?' asked Giuseppi doubtfully.

'She certainly can!' said Francesca snootily, going out with her nose in the air.

But then she reappeared.

'Butter?' she said anxiously.

'What did I –' began Giuseppi but Jalila cut across him quickly.

'I will help, Francesca,' she said. 'If I may. I would like to.'

'Make the one your father likes,' decreed Maria.

'I can do that,' said Francesca, relieved, and she and Jalila went off into the kitchen.

'Why isn't that girl like her mother?' asked Giuseppi. 'Julia always makes very fine cakes. She's good at cooking.'

'Francesca takes after you, that's why,' said Maria.

'Me?'

'Yes. Always arguing. With you it is all talk. And that is what she has learned from her grandfather. Instead of the useful things that I and her mother try to teach her.'

'It is true she questions things,' said Giuseppi. 'But is not that a good thing?'

'It is,' acknowledged Maria. 'Except that she tends to do it whenever I ask her to do something practical.'

'She helps out here,' objected Giuseppi.

'That's because she can talk while she cleans the dishes. No talk, nothing done. Like her grandfather.'

'I do sometimes worry what sort of a wife she will make,' confessed Giuseppi.

'The danger is no man will have her.'

'Giorgio likes her.'

'Even he gets restive when she keeps putting him right. And half the time he doesn't understand her. What she needs to do is marry a *professore*.'

'*Si, si!* A *professore* from the left!'

'They are always from the left,'said Maria tartly. 'That is why they have no money. And, talking of money –'

'I have given it you!' cried Giuseppi.

'No, no, it is not that. It is this pension of Jalila's.'

'It is good that it has come through.'

'Yes,' said Maria, 'but *why* has it come through? Now? After not having come through for so long?'

'It is because I went to the office and asked. I demanded. I said it was her right. As a widow of an –'

'Yes, yes,' said Maria impatiently. 'But who did you ask *with*?'

'You know. Rinaldo and Pietro. Why, you suggested –'

'I didn't suggest that Rinaldo tell them that Our Friends had an interest.'

'It was just to get them moving –'

'And that Rinaldo would go and talk to Our Friends afterwards.'

'That was just to make it right with them. So that they wouldn't think we were using their name without permission.'

'But you *were* using their name without permission.'

'They wouldn't mind! On a thing like this. If we told them.'

'No, they wouldn't mind, all right. They'll just send the bill in afterwards.'

'There's no question of money –'

'No. But perhaps there will be a question of repayment. What have you done, Giuseppi? What have you done?'

After breakfast Seymour went for a walk. His walk took him to the Porta del Carmine and the top of the street behind, the street down which, according to the *acquaiolo*, Scampion's murderer might have escaped. It was a street Seymour already knew – it was the one with the snail restaurant in – but now he looked at it anew in the light of what the *acquaiolo* had told him.

He saw a different Naples from the one he saw when he had looked out over the piazza. That one was broad and open and buzzing, filled with people and sunlight. The street on the other side of the Porta was narrow and dark and close, and although it, too, was congested, it was full of a different kind of life.

It was a working street, lined with *bassi*, the half workplace, half dwelling place, of the Neapolitan artisan. Things spilled out from the workshops: wood from the carpenters and turners, sheets of cork newly cut from the trees on the hills above the city, great sweeps of sailcloth spreading right across the street, blocking off the view; half-completed rush mats, wickerwork baskets and chairs still being worked on, their spokes pointing up into the air, low wooden racks filled with pipes in various stages of progress.

A man walking down the street – or, more probably, running – would be invisible within a few yards. Especially if, as the *acquaiolo* had suggested, he had gone into a *basso*.

110

And that would have been easy. Many of the *bassi* had half-doors like those of a coach house, which folded open and remained open all day. Often they opened on to the street, indeed, were often pulled half across the street, protruding like fences or walls and marking off not just the working space for each *basso* but also a kind of extra living space for the family. Children played there, the wife prepared her meals there. Elderly relatives sat there, for most of the day, moving only from sunshine in the early morning to shade at noon.

And, everywhere, hanging from windows and balconies, dangling sometimes into the *bassi* themselves, were clothes, newly washed and quickly drying, but almost at once, especially when, as was usual, there were small children in the family, as quickly replaced.

Hard, then, to see a man hurrying down the street.

And he might not even have been hurrying. He might have taken his time in a *basso* and then sauntered out some time later.

Even so, with all these people about, someone must have seen him. But how could Seymour prise that out of them? In London it would have been simple. ('Just making a few routine inquiries.') But here he was not a policeman, he was just a stranger casually chatting.

And in Italian, too! Seymour was fairly fluent in Italian but his command of the language wasn't quite up to this. For a start, the Italian they spoke in these back streets was not the Italian he knew. It was dialect, a Neapolitan language of its own. He had met it at the snail restaurant. The carpenter and the *acquaiolo* spoke it habitually. But they also spoke, and shifted into it for his benefit, a standard Italian. The people he tried speaking to in the street were nearly incomprehensible, especially if, as was often the case, their reply came from a mouth practically without teeth.

But that was not the most difficult part. The difficulty was that as soon as he got near the subject of the killing ('Just at the end of the street!') they clammed up. Was it, he wondered, simply the usual tactic of the poor, to keep your

111

mouth shut and your head down when something came along that might cause trouble? Or was it usual reaction of a close-knit community to a stranger and, especially, a foreigner? Or was it something else?

As he came out through the gate of the Porta he saw the Marchesa coming across the piazza towards him. She was with a group of smartly dressed young men.

'Why, Signor Seymour! How nice to see you!'

'And nice to see you, Marchesa!'

'You see,' the Marchesa said to the young men, 'he speaks Italian!'

'Why shouldn't he speak Italian?' one of them said.

'Because he's an Englishman. And a policeman. He has come out here to find out who killed Scampion.'

'I am here on holiday,' said Seymour. 'With my fiancée.'

'A most charming and beautiful woman,' said the Marchesa. 'I recommend you all to make her acquaintance. Especially as you seem to have mislaid your own fiancées.'

'It's no joke, Luisa,' said one of the men.

'You have left them behind, I know. To guard the hearth and await your return. But cannot you do as sailors are supposed to do? Why not have a fiancée in every port?'

'We might have other things on our mind when we get to Libya,' one of the men said. Seymour thought he recognized him. Umberto, was it? One of Vincente's bicycling friends.

He looked around, Vincente wasn't there. He could well have been, though. Seymour guessed that they were all young officers.

'Oh, you are serious!' said the Marchesa. 'But, then, you have just been to Mass.'

'So have you, Luisa,' one of them pointed out.

'No, not me,' said the Marchesa. 'I just went there for the singing.'

'I wish you wouldn't say things like that, Luisa!'

'That's the trouble with Mass: it depresses you for the day,' said the Marchesa.

Several of the men sighed.

'We have just been to a Mass,' the Marchesa told Seymour. 'For those going out to Libya, and for those who have already gone.'

'And for those who have already gone and now will stay there,' said one of the men quietly.

The Marchesa, conscious of the reproof, turned away and began talking to some of the other officers.

Two of them came up to Seymour.

'Is it true, Signor? That you are a policeman?'

'Yes.'

'And have come here to find out who killed Signor Scampion?'

'Among other things, yes.'

'I hope you do,' said the man he took to be Umberto. 'He was a good friend of ours.'

'A bicycling friend?'

'Not just a bicycling friend. We met in other ways, too. But not only here. We knew him in Florence.'

'And in Rome,' said the other young officer. 'I used to meet him at parties. But I didn't really get to know him until I got to Florence and he started to come to our meetings.'

'Meetings?'

'We used to meet regularly. A group of us. To discuss things. Serious things, I mean. Not just any old things. It wasn't just a social club.'

'What sort of things did you discuss?'

Umberto laughed. 'Life. Italy. Religion.'

'The big questions,' said his friend.

'You are not, by any chance, members of the Sursum Corda?'

'Well, yes, we are,' said Umberto, surprised. He turned to the other officer.

'Isn't that interesting?' he said. 'Here's another Englishman who knows about us.'

'Another? Scampion was the first, I take it. Was he actually a member?'

'Not a member, no. He couldn't be. There is a religious issue. But he used to come to our meetings.'

'He was a serious man,' said the other officer, 'and we hoped that in time he would come to see things as we did.'

'He saw so many things as we did,' said Umberto. 'It was surprising in an Englishman. Because the things seemed so deeply Italian. The need for Italy to raise its head again. And redeem itself.'

'After that disgraceful war!'

'The Abyssinian one?' said Seymour.

'Call it by its proper name,' said the other officer. 'Defeat: that's what it was.'

'And you hope that you can, perhaps, put that right through the war with Libya?'

'We *will* put it right.'

'In that case I *am* surprised. That Signor Scampion should identify so strongly with your cause.'

'We were surprised, too. But, you know, he was a man of generous enthusiasm. And I think he was fired in the way that we were fired. By the same ideals.'

'And by the same person.'

'The same person, yes.'

'We were fortunate in that our soirées were attended by a very remarkable man, a poet and a visionary.'

'Visionary, yes. He was certainly that. We were all inspired by him. And I think Signor Scampion was, too.'

'It wasn't just a narrow thing, you know.' said Umberto. 'Not just a question of Italy. It went much wider. It was a question of recognizing ideals and values that have been lost. And I think that struck a chord with Signor Scampion.'

'He was a good man.'

'I could hardly believe it when I heard.'

'These Neapolitan streets!'

'*And* when he was on an errand of mercy.'

'Errand of mercy?' said Seymour.

'So it appears. The lads were talking about it after the race last Saturday. You see, he had been out with us that morning, the morning he was killed. Normally, we have a glass afterwards, but this time he didn't want to. He said there was someone he had to see. "A lady?" someone said jokingly. "Yes, a lady," he said, but quite seriously.

'Of course, we all started teasing him. "No, it's not like that," he said. "It's something I've been asked to do. To help her."

'Of course, that didn't stop the teasing. But he wouldn't say any more. He just smiled, and then rode off. But afterwards, when we heard, we remembered it. And some of the boys felt we ought to look into it. But others said no, it was a private matter, perhaps even a question of a lady's honour. So we didn't. You haven't come across the lady in question, have you? In your investigations? Because if you have, and something has been left uncompleted, we'd like to know. If it's a question of money, say, we'd like to chip in. We feel we have a certain responsibility, you know. He was one of us. Almost.'

'It's going to be big,' announced Giorgio.

'If it happens at all,' said Giuseppi.

'Oh, it'll happen,' Giorgio assured him. 'Both sides have issued their challenges and somebody from the Reds is coming down today to approve the course.'

'The Yellows have an unfair advantage,' said Giuseppi. 'They know the course. In fact, they've been riding it for weeks.'

'The Reds know the course, too,' said Giorgio. 'They ride that way when they come down.'

'It's not the same thing,' said Giuseppi.

'No, it's not,' put in Maria unexpectedly. 'The Yellows have been racing it. The Reds have just been riding it.'

'Well, they seem to have accepted it,' said Giorgio. 'And if they don't like it, they can turn it down this afternoon.'

'There's a lot of interest in the race in Naples,' said Francesca.

'A lot of money put down on it, too, I'll bet,' said Maria.

'The fools!' sneered Giuseppi. 'They'll lose it all.'

'Only if they're betting on the Reds,' said Francesca.

'It's their duty to bet on the Reds!' said Giuseppi fiercely.

'It's your duty not to bet at all,' said Maria. 'How much money have you got? Give it to me!'

'I need some!' protested Giuseppi. 'For a cup of coffee.'

'For a glass of beer!' said Maria. 'No! Give me your money.'

Grumbling, Giuseppi turned out his pockets. Maria scooped up the change and took it away.

'I'll lend you some, Grandfather,' said Francesca. 'Then you can bet. You'll have to repay it, of course.'

'Well, that's not unreasonable.'

'At a suitable rate of interest.'

'Capitalist!' cried Giuseppi.

'Francesca, you cannot do this!' said Giorgio, shocked. 'Lend money to your grandfather at interest.'

'I lend to you, don't I?' said Francesca.

'Yes, but that's quite different.'

'I thought you were the man with money, Giorgio?' said Giuseppi slyly.

'I am,' said Giorgio. 'Only sometimes I am short.'

'Are *you* going to bet, Giorgio?' asked Giuseppi.

'Probably.'

'On the Yellows, I suppose?'

'My heart is with the Reds,' said Giorgio unctuously. 'However, my head is with the Yellows.'

'You'd do better to listen to your heart,' said Giuseppi.

'And lose my money? Actually,' said Giorgio, a little shame-facedly, 'I've already lost my money. I bet Lorenzo that a pigeon wouldn't shit on Pietro's head. He was standing just in front of the Palazzo, you see, where there's a lot of pigeons up on the pediment. I thought I was safe. Pigeons don't usually shit on people's heads. This one did.'

'Do you want me to lend you some money, Giorgio?' asked Francesca.

'Well –'

'At a suitable rate of interest,' said Giuseppi.

Francesca took some paper and began to write down calculations.

'What are you doing?'

116

'Deciding how much interest I'm going to charge. And what the odds are.'

'What!'

'Since I'm lending to both sides, I ought to be able to make a profit,' said Francesca, 'no matter who wins.'

'Jesus, Francesca!' said Giuseppi and Giorgio in unison.

Seymour was still thinking about how he was going to get information out of the inhabitants of the *bassi*. It wasn't just the language difficulty: it was also how he could somehow manage to outflank their suspicions. What he needed was some kind of pretext for asking his questions, a pretext which they would all understand and be sympathetic to.

At last he thought he had hit on it.

He went down the narrow street behind the Porta del Carmine until he came to the water shop. Like the snail restaurant, it was not so much a shop as a base. The *acquaiolo* had parked his wares in the middle of the street, just where the street took a useful bend and from where the *acquaiolo* would command the approaches in both directions, visible, and audible, to all.

His wares, like those of the snail-shop owner, again did not amount to much. They consisted of a huge tank which during the day was pulled out across the street, forcing the traffic to slow, and at night was pushed back against the wall. The tank contained the *acquaiolo*'s working supply of water for the day and fed a small urn from which he actually supplied his customers. The urn stood on a little table and was lovingly polished every day. In front of it was a row of enamel cups. Beneath the table were the goatskins in which the *acquaiolo* fetched his water, in the morning on a small donkey, during the day on a yoke carried across his shoulders.

He greeted Seymour with a big smile.

'How are things?' he said.

Seymour took him by the arm, looked up and down the street, bent closer and said, in a low voice: 'I'm working on it.'

'Working on . . .?'

'The numbers. I've been thinking over what we said. It was so close that I think I could be almost there. There must be just some tiny feature that I've not allowed for. Something I've not taken into account on the numbering.'

'What is it?'

'That's just the trouble!' said Seymour. 'I don't know. But what I've come round to thinking is that it must be something to do with what happened on that day, the day the Englishman was killed. It could be anything. The last person the man met as he was running away afterwards. A *basso* that he went into. Children – could it be anything to do with children, do you think? I mean, they're all over the place. That could be significant.'

'Well, it could,' said the *acquaiolo* doubtfully. 'But –'

'You see, that's the problem. I just don't know. It could be anything. So I've got to ask around. What I feel is that if I hit on it, it would jump out at me. It would sort of announce itself.'

'Well, it might,' said the *acquaiolo*. 'But –'

'What I feel I've got to do is ask around. Generally, because it might be anything. I'd like to ask people if they remembered anything about that day. Anything that stood out. Or, perhaps, did not stand out particularly. Just anything. But details. I feel it's got to be a detail, something particular. That's what the number's looking for, isn't it? It's got to be some detail that makes it stand out from other numbers.'

'Well, yes, I suppose –'

'But if I go down the street asking people for any details that they remember from that day, they'll think I'm loony, won't they? But if I could find a way of letting people know why I'm doing it, they might be sympathetic.'

'Oh, I think they would! But you mustn't tell them too much, you know, or they'll all be doing it.'

'Oh, I don't want to tell them too much. I won't tell them anything specific. Just that I'm trying to look for a number.'

'I think they'll certainly be interested. And I'm pretty sure they'll want to help, once they know.'

'But, you see,' said Seymour, 'I'm worried because I'm a stranger here. I was wondering if you would mind putting in a word for me. Just let them know what I'm doing and why I'm doing it.'

'I'd be glad to,' said the *acquaiolo*.

Just at that moment the carpenter appeared, on his way to the snail restaurant, and they decided to go with him.

Seymour explained the situation.

The carpenter understood it at once.

'You're right,' he said. 'The number is a good number. I've said that from the start. It just needs something adding. And it's got to be a particular, hasn't it? I mean, it would be no good if it was just "a man". It's got to be a particular man.'

'That's why I thought: a man running away,' said Seymour.

But it didn't bite.

'Of course, it doesn't have to be a man,' said *acquaiolo*. 'It could be a woman. Your wife, for instance,' he said to the carpenter.

'No, I don't think so,' said the carpenter.

'It could!' the *acquaiolo* insisted. 'Theoretically, I mean,' he added hastily.

'No, I don't think so,' said the carpenter. 'And I'll tell you why. The number has got to fit in with the other numbers. And my wife wouldn't fit in with anything.'

'The other thing it could be,' said Seymour, lowering his voice, 'although I don't quite know how to get this in, and maybe it's best not to go down that route anyway, is –'

He dropped his voice to the merest whisper, so that they had to put their heads in close to him.

'– Our Friends.'

They started back.

'No,' said the carpenter hastily. 'No, I really don't think –'

'Best not to go down that route,' said the *acquaiolo*.

'Well, I wouldn't,' said Seymour. 'But if you think about it, it's not such a bad idea.'

'It's a very bad idea,' said the carpenter.

119

'But that's just the point,' said Seymour. 'Everyone knows it's a bad idea. So maybe it's a good one.'

'I'm not sure that I'm altogether following you,' said the carpenter.

'No one else is going to go down that road, are they?' said Seymour. 'And maybe that's what the number wants. Otherwise it would be paying off for everybody.'

'Yes, well, I still think it's a bad idea,' said the carpenter.

The *acquaiolo*, however, was becoming more enthusiastic.

'You could be on to something,' he said thoughtfully. 'It has to be something special doesn't it? And Our Friends –'

'Just keep your voice down a bit,' said the carpenter.

'– are certainly special.'

'Yes, but –'

'The more you think about it,' said Seymour.

'I know, but –'

'You see, I reckon I'm on the right track with the rest of the number. It just needs one other thing. But that thing must be big, mustn't it? A small number in itself but big in importance. And that would fit. If you know what I mean.'

'I know what you mean,' said the carpenter, 'and I think it's best to drop it.'

'But is it?' said Seymour. 'Is it? Not from the point of view of winning, I mean, but from the point of view of politeness.'

'What?' said the *acquaiolo*.

'Politeness?' said the carpenter.

'Well yes. To Our Friends, I mean. I wouldn't want to insult them. And wouldn't it be insulting them to leave them out? If they, by any chance, were a factor, I mean.'

'The number would be incomplete,' said the *acquaiolo* thoughtfully.

'That's it. It would be an insult to Our Friends *and* to the number!'

'That certainly is a consideration!'

'But how,' said the carpenter, beginning to be convinced, 'how could you fit them in? I mean, what number could you give them?'

'Look it up in the book,' said the *acquaiolo*.

'But it won't *be* in the book, will it? You don't put that sort of number in a book, not in Naples.'

'Number one?' suggested the *acquaiolo*.

'That would be a good number for them,' acknowledged the carpenter. 'But it's been used already. *Everyone* in Naples puts that number down.'

'The way I see it,' said Seymour, 'is that it's no good thinking of a number that anyone would know refers to Our Friends. That would take care of the politeness, all right. But it wouldn't help us with the number. It's got to be more specific. What we want is something we can give a number to which links them to what happened by the Porta del Carmine.'

'Like what?'

'Well, I don't know,' confessed Seymour. 'But I feel that if I cast around, the number will leap up and hit me.'

'This is getting a bit deep for me,' said the *acquaiolo*.

'Me, too,' said the carpenter. 'My head is beginning to reel.'

'So is mine,' said Seymour. 'Let's give it a rest. But, you know, I think we're on the right lines. It's just a case of hitting on the right number.'

'It always is,' sighed the *acquaiolo*.

Chapter Nine

Chantale had returned to the *pensione* and was sitting outside on the patio reading a book. She heard a door inside the house open and close and then the young man, Bruno, came out on to the patio.

'Your pardon, Signora!' he said, jumping back with a start when he saw Chantale.

'It is nothing,' said Chantale, smiling. 'Can I help you?'

'I was looking for Jalila,' said the young man hesitantly.

'Ah! She has just gone out for the moment with Maria to get the bread. She will be back – oh, at any moment now.'

'Thank you. I will wait, then.'

He was about to go back into the house, then wavered.

'Do you mind, Signora . . .?'

He indicated a spare chair on the patio.

'Not at all.'

He sat down.

'I do not like to wait in the kitchen,' he said. 'Not when Maria is not there. And Francesca doesn't seem to be there, either.'

'She is not yet back from school.'

He looked at his watch, a large, rather good one.

'No, of course not!' he said. 'She wouldn't be. School goes on longer than in my day. And Francesca, I know, does extra.'

He shook his head.

'Although I don't see the point of that,' he said. 'What can it lead to? Especially in the case of a girl. What work can she do? Oh, work in the home. Yes, helping Maria, or perhaps Julia. Or even in a shop, although, personally, I think that with so many men out of work, girls ought not to take the jobs that are going. But the teachers say she is very clever and Giuseppi says she must have her chance. But chance to do what, I ask myself? It is, perhaps, different in your country,' he said hastily.

Perhaps. But which was her country? England, or Morocco? In England, certainly, there were jobs for women. Seymour's own sister, whom she had met and whom she liked, was a teacher. But in Tangier . . .!

She laughed to herself, and then saw Bruno looking at her.

'In Tangier, no,' she said. 'In London, yes.'

'You come from Tangier?'

'In the first place, yes.'

'But now you live in London. With Signor Seymour.'

'Yes.'

'That is how I would wish it to be for Jalila.'

'You think it better for her to be here than with her family in Libya?'

'Oh, yes! Here,' he said, waving a hand largely. 'Here are jobs, opportunities.'

Despite what he had just said.

'Perhaps for the children,' said Chantale, 'when they grow up. But it is not so easy for her.'

'No, no, indeed. It is very difficult.' He hesitated. 'It is not just that she is a woman, Signora. It is that she is an Arab. It is wrong, I know, but people are prejudiced about Arabs. It is the war partly, but not just that. People say, what is she doing here? And why does she bring extra mouths to feed when there is barely enough in Naples? I do not say that. For me, it is enough that she was married to Tonio.'

'You and he were very close, I gather?'

'Very close.'

He held out his hand with his first two fingers close together.

'Like that,' he said. 'You do not, perhaps, understand how it is for Italians, Signora. At least, how it is for

123

Neapolitans. We were like blood brothers. We would always do things together. We played together, worked together. Until he went into the army. Even then I would have gone with him, but my mother was old and sick and alone, and Tonio said, you cannot. It would not be right. So I stayed and he went.'

He looked at Chantale.

'But do you know what?' he said. 'He sent his first pay packet home to me. For her. He knew how poor we were.'

He was silent for a moment.

'People ask,' he went on, 'why do you do so much for an Arab woman? I say, because he would have done the same for me. How can I not do this? It is not for her I do it but for him.'

'It is praiseworthy,' said Chantale, 'whoever it be for.'

She hesitated, wondering whether she should say more, and then decided, since he seemed to have confidence in her, that she would risk it.

'But, Bruno,' she said, 'are there not limits to what you should do for her? They tell me you wish to marry her.'

'Tonio would have done the same for me,' Bruno said seriously.

'No doubt. But – but, Bruno, marriage is a complex business, and many things come into it. You have to be sure that it is wanted on her side.'

'Of course!'

'And she may wish to choose for herself.'

Bruno laughed. 'That is what women always say, Signora. But women are realists, too. They are realistic as well as romantic. Otherwise it is like an opera. And life in Naples, Signora, is not like an opera. There is not much choosing to be done. For men, it is either the army or poverty. For women, it is poverty or marriage. And if you are a widow with children, well . . .!'

He made a dismissive gesture with his hand.

Chantale wondered whether she would persist. She felt that she was coming up against bedrock Neapolitan, or perhaps even Italian, attitudes. Or – possibly Bruno was right – bedrock Neapolitan realities. To her they seemed not just rock, they seemed terribly tangled and confused. She had often thought that men's attitudes in Tangier were tangled and confused, but that seemed as nothing compared with how things were in Naples.

Or maybe that was how it always seemed when you were looking at a society from outside?

'I know what you are thinking, Signora,' Bruno said seriously. 'You are thinking that perhaps it will be different because she is an Arab. You will know about this, Signora, because you yourself are an Arab. I realize it will be hard for her – it *is* hard for her. But that, you see, is why it is best if I marry her. Then she will not be alone. She will have a place in society and a man to stand by her. A woman needs that in Naples, Signora, and she needs it all the more if she comes from outside. And even more if she is black. And I will do that, Signora. Other men blow hot and cold. But not me, Signora. What I say I will do, I do.'

'I am sure of that, Bruno,' said Chantale. 'I know that you will stand by her and cherish her. But – I think that may not be all that she wants.'

Bruno looked puzzled.

'It will be difficult, I know, he said. 'That is what Alessandro said when we put it to him.'

'Alessandro?'

'He is a big cheese in Rome. He helped us to bring her back. "You daft bastards," he said. "Do you know what you are doing? She'll stand out like a sore thumb. She'll never feel right and never be right. She'd be better off in her own country. How will she manage in Naples? Tell me that! No man, no money. What do you think she is going to live on?"

'"Marcello says there will be a pension," I said. "Pension, pooh!" he said. "It won't be enough for her to buy a plate of spaghetti." "Our people will look after her," said Marcello. "Your people cannot even look after themselves," said Alessandro. "With two children? Two extra mouths? That's a lot in a family. Just ask me! I know. Listen, I know about this. I was poor in Naples myself once!"

'"Tonio would have wished it," I said.

125

'In the end he agreed. "All right, all right!" he said. "I'll do it. Since he was from Naples, and you're from Naples, and I'm from Naples. Okay! I'll do it. But it's madness, I tell you, madness! You boys are never going to get anywhere in life. You've got to be tougher, harder. Learn to put things behind you. You can't afford to take on things. Things you can't pay for. Like my wife, for example. Jesus! Have I learnt it the hard way! It's like running the National Debt. She *is* the National Debt! Get out while you still can. That's my advice to you. Don't take on things you cannot finish."

'"Tonio would have wished it."

'"All right, all right. I'll pay for her to come to Naples. And the kids. Christ, we can't leave them behind, can we? Although, come to think of it, maybe we should. No? All right, then, kids as well. But, mind you, once she's in Naples, I wash my hands of them. From then on she's your lookout. I want nothing more to do with it. Do you hear?"

'Well, we heard, all right. That's the way these big cheeses talk. It doesn't mean anything. But he did bring her back. His bank paid for it. He's got a bank, you see, the Bank of Rome. And he was setting up this branch in Libya. And Marcello got to hear of it and heard that he came from Naples. So he wrote to me and said, this is the answer. You see, we couldn't do it ourselves. Not even between us. We hadn't the money and he told me to go to Alessandro.

'So I went to Alessandro and said: "I want some help, and I think you're a cousin of mine." "I don't have any cousins in Naples," said Alessandro. "That's one thing I've learnt. And that's one thing you'd better learn if you want to get on. Cousins are like locusts. They eat everything you've got. Anyway, you're not a cousin."

'Well, it was true. He wasn't a cousin of mine. But, Christ, everyone in Naples is pretty well related, and he might have been. And I reckoned Alessandro wouldn't know. Well, of course, he didn't. Who the hell knows what his father has been up to, let alone his uncles? But he knew he came from Naples and thought it might be true. And,

126

apparently, or so Marcello said, he had a soft spot for Naples. So he listened.

'And I told him the whole story, about Tonio. "This is one hell of a daft bastard," said Alessandro. "First, he volunteers for the army. Then he goes to Libya. And then marries an Arab woman. You can't do anything for a man like that."

'"I'm not asking you to do anything for him," I say. "He's dead. What I am asking you to do is something for his widow. And it's not much money to someone like you. And it's important to me. And to Tonio. And to Tonio's mate in Libya." "Christ, another one!" says Alessandro. "I told you they were like locusts." "This isn't just another one," I say. "He was like a brother to him." "Oh, yes?" says Alessandro. "Yes," I say, "a blood brother. Sworn. And I'm like that, too. So you've got to do something." "Because I come from Naples?" says Alessandro. "Yes. And because you've got on and we haven't."

'"Naples," says Alessandro, "is like a bloody great weight you've got around your neck. You never get rid of it."

'All the same, he agreed to pay for Jalila.'

'I *have* got a job!' protested Giorgio indignantly. 'In fact, I've got three.'

'Three?'

'One at the baker's. I help Luigi with the morning round.'

'Sometimes,' said Giuseppi.

'Three days a week. It's regular. And I get paid for it.'

'Next to nothing,' said Giuseppi.

'It's better than nothing,' said Giorgio hurt.

'It *is* better than nothing, Giorgio,' said Maria. 'And it helps your mother. You're a good boy, Giorgio. But it won't go far if you're thinking of marriage.'

'Who's thinking of marriage?'

'You are,' said Francesca. 'Or you ought to be.'

127

'When you leave school, Francesca,' said Maria firmly, 'then will be the time to think of marriage.'

'I'm planning ahead,' said Francesca sulkily.

'Yes, well, you can plan without me,' said Giorgio. 'I'm not thinking of marriage.'

'Yet,' said Francesca.

'Yet,' Giorgio agreed. 'Nor for a long time,' he added hastily.

'It will be a long time if all you've got to marry on is three mornings at the baker's,' said Giuseppi.

'What's the other job, Giorgio?' asked Maria.

'I help Gianni with the barrels,' said Giorgio.

'Twice a week,' said Giuseppi.

'It's something,' said Giorgio.

'It certainly is,' agreed Maria. 'But, Giorgio, it doesn't go far.'

'I don't throw my money around,' said Giorgio.

'He certainly doesn't,' said Francesca. 'Look how he's saved up for that bicycle.'

'I've seen that bicycle before,' said Giuseppi, 'several times. In other people's hands.'

'Not everyone around here has got a bicycle,' said Giorgio. 'In fact, I'm the only one. And the point is that now I can ride to work. That brings other jobs within reach.'

'There!' said Francesca. 'Doesn't that show how ambitious he is?'

'What other jobs!' asked Giuseppi. 'There aren't any out there, either.'

'Oh, yes, there are,' said Giorgio smugly. 'And I've got one.'

'You've got one?' said Maria.

'Oh, Giorgio, you didn't tell me!' said Francesca, delighted. 'Where is it?'

'Over at the base. The army base.'

'You've not done anything daft, have you?' said Giuseppi. 'Like enlisted?'

'I'm too young,' said Giorgio. 'Still. Although when I am old enough, I certainly will,' he said defiantly. 'I know you

128

don't like it, Giuseppi, but for me it's the way out. It will only be for a short time and then I'll have enough money to start a bicycle shop.'

'There!' said Francesca. 'You see?'

'I can see him getting a hole in his head,' said Giuseppi.

'Giuseppi! Do not say such things!' said Maria. 'It's bad luck.'

'And at least he's doing *something*,' said Francesca. 'That's what you always say, Grandfather. That's what you say people should do. Get off their asses and do something.'

'Francesca, I will not have you using such language!'

'It's not my language, it's Grandfather's.'

'I won't have *him* using it, either,' said Maria.

'What is this job, then, Giorgio?' asked Francesca. 'The one you've got at the base.'

'It's a temporary one only,' Giorgio confessed. 'But they say it could lead to something. And, anyway, they say it will help when I put my name down for the army. It's cleaning the bicycles and getting them ready for the big race on Saturday.'

'They pay you for *that*?' said Giuseppi.

'They certainly do. And will. Better than I get at the baker's or with the barrels. More than Luigi makes during the whole week! He told me so himself.'

'These rich men can afford it,' said Giuseppi.

'It's a kindness to take their money from them. You say that, too, Giuseppi.'

'It depends on the circumstances,' muttered Giuseppi.

'There you are! You see!' said Francesca. 'The money is rolling in. Soon he will be able to think of marriage.'

'Now, hold it, Francesca!' said Giuseppi, Maria and Giorgio.

'So you're working at the army base, now, Giorgio?' said Seymour, after Giuseppi and Maria had left.

'That's right.'

'You're pretty busy, I expect, with the big race about to come off?'

'I am. I shall be busy on the day, too. They're paying me extra for that. They want me to wash their bicycles down afterwards. But I've got a problem.'

'What's the problem?' asked Francesca.

'Water. Where am I going to get all that water from? It'll have to come from the pump, I suppose, but that's a long way away. And I'll be getting through the water at a fantastic rate.'

'Get someone to bring it.'

'Oh, yes!' said Giorgio. 'And by the time I've paid them to do that, there'll be no money left for me!'

'One of the officers, Vincente, is arranging for some water to be brought,' said Seymour.

'Oh, yes, but that's for drinking.'

'Couldn't you use some of that?'

'That will be being paid for and they might not be very keen to have it used on washing bicycles down.'

Giorgio looked at Francesca.

'I've been wondering about Jalila,' he said.

'Getting her to fetch the water?'

'Yes. She'll be glad of the work.'

'It would have to be paid for,' said Francesca doubtfully. 'You couldn't expect her to do it for nothing.'

'Well, I wouldn't mind paying Jalila. A bit. I mean, I wouldn't have to pay her as much as I would a man.'

'There's not going to be much money in this for you, Giorgio, if you're paying her something. However small,' said Francesca. 'And would she do it, anyway?'

'Oh, I think she would,' said Giorgio confidently. 'She's interested in bicycles.'

'What!' said Seymour.

'Jalila?' said Chantale.

'Are you sure?' said Francesca doubtfully.

'Yes!' Giorgio insisted. 'I've often seen her talking to the Signor.'

'What Signor is this?'

'The English Signor.'

130

'Signor Scampion?'

'Yes. I used to see him talking to her at the Porta del Carmine after he'd been out riding.'

'You're sure it was them?' said Seymour.

'Look,' said Giorgio, 'an Arab woman and an Englishman! You don't make mistakes over that.'

'I'm sure you saw them, Giorgio,'said Chantale, 'but . . .'

She hesitated. 'Giorgio, are you sure they were talking about bicycles?'

'Yes,' snapped Francesca. 'He's quite sure!'

'He always had his bicycle with him,' said Giorgio, a little lost, 'and I think he was showing it to her. What else would they be talking about?'

'Giorgio, we have to go now,' said Francesca, hustling him away.

'In my family's house,' said Jalila, 'there was always water.'

She and Chantale were sitting on the patio at the back of the *pensione*. The smaller child was asleep on Jalila's lap. The little girl had just been sitting on Chantale's lap being read to but they had come to the end of the story and she had slipped off Chantale's knee and taken the book to the other side of the patio, where she was now sitting turning the pages and looking at the pictures by herself.

The book was a children's book, which was why Chantale had noticed it. There weren't many books for children in Arabic. She didn't think she had ever seen one. There were religious prohibitions against the representation of human forms and although in some parts of the Muslim world it was quite common to represent animals and flowers and trees, among the stricter Muslims even that was frowned on. So she had been intrigued when she had picked this book up.

'Where did you get it from?' she had asked.

'It is a special book,' said Jalila. 'Tonio and Marcello found it when they were out together one day in Benghazi. Marcello was always interested in books – Tonio less so – and they went in. The owner was a Jew and he had lots of interesting books, some of them in Italian. There was only one, though, that was for children, and Marcello picked it out. It was the pictures, I think, which struck him. They were, he said, as a child would draw. Well, now, most of our children do not draw, so I wouldn't know.

'But Marcello said: "Your children would like this, Tonio." And so he bought it for him as a present. Tonio was not sure about this because in his own house in Naples there were no books, and he himself didn't read much. But in Marcello's house there *were* books and both Giuseppi and Maria made much of them.

'"If your children are going to grow up as Italians," Marcello said, "they must grow up as *real* Italians. And not just *real* Italians, but *rich* Italians. It will not do, Tonio, for either your children or my children to grow up as we have done. For them it must be better. And so I will buy this book for you."

'Which he did. So this book, Signora, is special. It speaks to me of my husband and his friend. And it speaks also of all our hopes. Some of those hopes, Signora,' said Jalila, 'can now never be fulfilled. My husband is dead. But others of them, his, and mine, and, yes, Marcello's, too, *will* be fulfilled. This I have sworn, Signora, and I will keep my oath.'

'It is right that parents should wish the best for their children,' said Chantale. 'As I expect your parents did for you.'

'Yes,' said Jalila, laughing, 'and when I told them I wished to marry Tonio, they were not sure it had happened!'

'Who knows?' said Chantale. 'In the end you may have great joy from your children.'

'Yes,' said Jalila, laughing, 'and no doubt great trouble also!'

She gave them a fond look.

'But, meanwhile,' she said, 'if they are to eat, I have to fetch water.'

'Even with the pension?'

'Even with the pension,' said Jalila. 'The water will perhaps buy them some treats which otherwise they would not have known. The difference between eating and eating well is as little as that.'

She sighed. 'And so, Signora, I have to think hard. If, as Marcello said, it is not enough for our children to grow up as we did, then I have to think very hard. Carrying water will not bring that about. And so, Signora, I come back again to Bruno, who was, too, a good friend of Tonio's.'

'But you hesitate,' said Chantale.

'Yes,' said Jalila, 'I hesitate. And it is not because I think like a maid, Signora. I am past that. It is . . .'

She stopped, and rocked the child a little on her lap.

'Bruno is a good man,' she said. 'He is good to his mother and he would be good to me and to them. But although he is a good man, Signora, and is earning good money, he does not earn his money in a good way.'

'How does he earn it?'

'He collects,' said Jalila simply.

'Collects?'

But Jalila wouldn't say more.

The little boy on her lap stirred and Jalila bent over him and stroked his cheek. He half opened his eyes and she stroked them shut and began to croon a little baby song. He went back to sleep and she sat quietly rocking him.

On the other side of the patio the little girl read on determinedly.

'Jalila,' said Chantale, 'have others tried to help you?'

'Oh, yes,' said Jalila. 'Tonio's family, and Maria and Giuseppi –'

'I wasn't talking about them,' said Chantale. 'I was talking about people – people not from Naples.'

'My patron, you mean? The man who paid for me to come back from Libya to Naples. Marcello and Bruno say that I must always be grateful to him, and I am.'

'And has he helped you since?'

Jalila hesitated.

'Yes,' she said, 'although he swore he would not. He sent me some money. It is all spent, though. I had to spend it when the pension did not come through. He sent it me by the Englishman.'

'Signor Scampion?'

'Yes. The nice Englishman.'

'And was it just the once that he sent you money?'

'Yes. But, as he said, he had already done much for me.'

'It is said,' Chantale chose her words carefully, 'it is said, Jalila, that the Englishman saw you more than once. In fact, that he saw you several times.'

'Ah, yes, but that was not to give me money.'

'No?'

'No. That was –' She stopped, then continued. 'That was because my patron had asked him to keep on eye on me and see that all was well. He used to give me words of comfort, for which I was very grateful.'

'And this was all?'

'All? Well, as I have said, my patron had said there could be no question of money –'

'Was there more to it than that, Jalila?'

'More to it?'

'Because people say there was.'

Jalila flushed angrily.

'People will say these things,' she snapped, 'whether there be truth in them or no.'

'And there was no truth in them?'

Jalila did not reply for a moment.

'Perhaps there was,' she said then. 'A little. But only a little. We met, perhaps, more often that we should have done. But it was, I think, a comfort to us both. For me, because even with all the good people around me, I still, at times, felt very alone. And I think he felt alone, too. At times. He was, like me, a stranger in a strange land. And he needed to talk to someone, he said, who was also a stranger. Or, at least, someone who was not Italian, for the Italians were blinded, as he had been.

'Besides, he said, he wanted to talk to someone who knew what war meant. Not what war *was* – a soldier, any soldier, could tell him that, provided he had served. He said that the young men at the base had not previously served yet, they had not yet been on the battlefield, and so they did not really know.

'But, in any case, he said, that was not what he wanted. What he wanted to know was what war *meant*. And for that, he said, he had to go to someone else, someone who had been touched by war and yet not been part of it. And for that, he said, he needed someone like me.

'I did not really understand him but I knew he meant well and that this was important to him. So we met and talked. And perhaps something grew out of that, or was beginning to grow out of that. But it never came to anything, we just talked. But the talking was important, and so we talked on.

'I think now that perhaps this was important to me, too, for I, too, did not understand what war meant. I did not understand what war had done to me – no, I knew that all right. But I did not know *why* it had done it to me, why it should have singled me out, as it seemed to have done.

'And he seemed to understand that, in a way that others didn't.'

She shrugged. 'So, well, we talked, and then he died. He was killed, like my husband. And I could not understand that, either. Why did this sort of thing happen to me? Was there something special about me, that I drew such things? Why should God have designed it thus? Or perhaps God had not designed it thus? Perhaps it had just happened. But if that was so, did that not mean that God did not design everything in the world, and how could that be? I felt I needed to talk to some learned man, but there was no learned man like that around here.

'I had said that to Signor Scampion and he said that no man was learned enough to be able to answer such questions. But that it was man's fate, and perhaps woman's fate especially, to ask such questions. And I could understand that, and especially about it being woman's fate, to ask them.'

Chapter Ten

When Chantale walked down the street there were always cries of *'Bellissima!'* from the young men lounging at every corner. At first she was taken aback and shrank into herself. But then she grew rather to like it. They were cries of appreciation not of incipient aggression; and she soon realized that she was not alone in receiving them. *Any* pretty girl in Neapolitan streets received the same treatment. It was not so much, as she had initially supposed, sexual ravenousness as a genuine admiration for beauty. Almost aesthetic, she thought. Almost.

Anyway, it was not like this in London; and it certainly was not like it in Tangier. In Tangier it would at once have produced a riot. The knives would have been out in a flash. Any male relative would have looked upon it as an insult which he was bound, for the sake of family honour, and for the sake of his own, to avenge.

Even in the East End of London, where she and Seymour lived, it was a bit like that. Very many of the people there were immigrants – Seymour himself came from an immigrant family (the 'Seymour' came from Shakespeare, chosen by a literature-loving Polish grandfather). They brought with them to London attitudes to family honour, and often to the females in their family, that were sometimes not so very different from those in Arab Morocco. Recourse was had less often to knives but if the girl of the family stepped out of line she would pretty swiftly be pulled back behind it. Or so Seymour's sister had informed Chantale. She herself, she said, had stepped out once or twice, and whenever she did, she said bitterly, there had been a hell of a to-do.

Seymour's own attitude was relaxed as it was on most things, but Chantale had noticed that he frequently bridled at the shouts of 'Bellissima', as if the sense of primitive male honour and possessiveness was not entirely absent; and she was rather pleased.

So when at the snail restaurant discussion began on the physical merits of a lady with whom they were obviously all familiar, she knew what to expect. Seymour was now, of course, a habitué of the restaurant, and Chantale had taken to dropping in with him. She was the only woman ever present and they treated her with an elaborate, old-fashioned courtesy which she rather enjoyed. Their own wives, of course, were never there.

The acquaiolo had seen the lady in question the previous day.

'And she is still as beautiful,' he said admiringly, 'as she ever was.'

'That sort of beauty never fades,' said the snail-restaurant owner sentimentally.

'It sort of deepens,' said the carpenter, which rather surprised Seymour, as he had never thought that the carpenter had a poetic side.

'Of course, when she was here, she was very young,' said the acquaiolo. 'Barely more than sixteen when I first heard her.'

'Heard her?' said Seymour.

'A wonderful voice!' said the snail-shop man sighing.

'Of course, it ripened with the years,' said the acquaiolo. 'But when I first heard her, it was as clear as a bell.'

'What did you first hear her in?' asked the carpenter.

'Mozart. I don't regard that as proper opera, but the freshness of the part suited her. Suited her as she was then, I should say. Of course, as she matured she went on to proper parts.'

'And then the bastards took her away,' said the snail man, sighing.

'She came back sometimes,' said the carpenter. 'She always had a soft spot for Naples.'

'Whenever she did, the crowds *outside* the house were immense. Never mind the crowd inside.'

'She was our girl,' said the snail man, sighing again.

'Whenever she came, Naples was all a-buzz,' said the carpenter.

'You couldn't get a ticket. They say not even Our Friends could get you one. At any price.'

'Ah, those were the days,' said the restaurant owner, concealing his emotion by dipping another portion into everybody's bowl.

'Do you still go to the opera?' asked Seymour, surprised; surprised because in London when you went to the opera, you didn't normally find yourself rubbing shoulders with carpenters and water-carriers or even restaurant owners.

'I try to see everything they put on here,' said the carpenter matter-of-factly.

The others nodded.

'Of course, it's got more expensive,' said the *acquaiolo*. 'The prices now are ridiculous.'

'That's what she said!'

They smiled in recollection.

'She came down here once and looked at the prices, and then she demanded that for one night they all be lowered. "So that her friends could come." And they did.'

'And I went,' said the carpenter. 'And she sang encore after encore, and the crowd was ecstatic. It went on till two in the morning.'

'That is the sort of woman she was,' said the snail man. 'We'll never see her like again.'

'We'll never *hear* her like again. She was remarkable. No wonder they spirited her away to La Scala.'

'But then she stopped. Quite suddenly.'

'Her voice was beginning to go, I think,' said the carpenter. 'She couldn't quite hit the top ones any more. "This is the time to go," she said. "Before it gets any worse. And while I'm still there."'

'It helped having a rich husband. She didn't need to work any more.'

'They say that when she married, he told her that in future she was to sing for him alone.'

'Those rich men are like that,' said the carpenter.

'Bastards!' said the *acquaiolo*.

'Shut her up like a bird in a cage. And hung the cage inside the house so no one else could hear her.'

'You know,' said the snail-shop owner, 'I don't think you could have seen her yesterday.'

'I did,' the *acquaiolo* insisted. 'I looked up, and there she was! As near to me as you are. I nearly dropped my water bags. In fact, I must have said something, for she turned round to me and smiled. And I'll tell you what: I may be old, and nine-tenths round the bend, but once you've seen it you never forget a smile like that. I used to hang around the stage door hoping to catch a sight of her. She used to come out and give everyone a smile – you know, a sort of we're-all-in-this-together smile, as if you were *sharing* something with her. You never forget a smile like that, I can tell you.'

'Ah, *bellissima*!' they all sighed in unison.

'Are you trying to tell me something?' demanded Chantale.

'Tell you something? No. What makes you think that?'

'This going to the Foundling Hospital: you're not hinting at something, are you?'

'Like what?'

'Like perhaps we should be thinking of adopting a child from there.'

'Good heavens, no!'

'No, well, I didn't really think you were. If we're going to have a child, we'll damned well have one of our own.'

'Never for one moment did I think that!'

'No, well, I didn't really think you did. What I thought was that this was an untypically subtle way of bringing pressure on me.'

'Pressure on you?' said Seymour, astonished.

'To marry. If it is, forget about it. I'm still making up my mind.'

'Listen, I just wanted to go back to the Foundling Hospital so that I could make the obvious check.'

'On?'

'Margareta. The Marchesa. To see if they're the same person.'

'So you were just thinking about this blasted case? You weren't thinking about us at all?'

'No.'

'I don't know why I'm even considering marrying you!'

'I would like to see Sister Geneviève,' said Seymour.

The nun hesitated.

'I don't know if she will see you,' she said. 'She is very frail now, and she has good days and bad days. Often, these days, she doesn't like to be bothered. What was it you wanted to see her about?'

'Margareta Esposito,' said Seymour. 'Just tell her that, will you?'

'Margareta!' said Sister Geneviève fondly. 'I can still hear her voice. Do you know her?'

'I have met her recently. At least, I think I have. We are not talking about a Marchesa, by any chance, are we?'

'Yes. She has been called to a great position, but I am sure she is worthy of it.'

'I am sure she is. But, alas, she has given up her singing.'

Sister Geneviève shook her head.

'That is wrong,' she said. 'She should not hide the talent that God has given her.'

'It is said that she has done so to please her husband.'

Sister Geneviève frowned. 'Her husband should not have asked such a thing of her.'

'There may be more to it than that. It is said, too, that her voice is not what it was.'

140

'That I will not believe!' said Sister Geneviève indignantly.

'Time passes,' said Seymour, 'and perhaps even Margareta is not immune.'

'But she is still young!' Sister Geneviève stopped and caught herself. 'Perhaps not so young now,' she admitted. 'It was all so long ago,' she said softly.

'Time creeps up on you,' said Seymour, 'and I think she felt it had crept up on her. Or was going to creep up on her. And she was not going to have it!'

Sister Geneviève laughed. 'That sounds like Margareta! She was never one to go out tamely.'

'I think she feared that her voice might be going and so she stopped. Before it did go. I think she wanted to go out while she was still at her best.'

'That would be Margareta, too,' said Sister Geneviève. 'She could never bear to be thought anything other than superb.'

Chantale laughed.

'I have met her, too,' she said, 'and I think I like her better in your description than I do in life.'

'She was never easy,' Sister Geneviève admitted.

'You know,' said Seymour, 'there is one thing that puzzles me. I know her as, and you speak of her as, a Marchesa. But the man she is married to is not noble. Not by birth, certainly. And I am not sure he has a title.'

'She married again,' said Sister Geneviève. 'That is not good, either, not according to God's laws. But, you know, I sometimes think – and, please, do not tell anyone here this – that a great spirit can somehow wriggle through God's laws.'

'So her title comes from her former husband?'

'Yes. The newspapers made a great thing of it at the time. "From foundling to Marchesa!" the headlines read. I don't think she was altogether pleased and nor was her husband, and certainly not her husband's family. She liked to keep that part of her life quiet. She was wrong to be ashamed of her beginnings, but I can understand it.'

Thinking about it, and about the girl she had once known, she smiled to herself and went into a daydream. And then, suddenly she fell asleep.

They rose to go, but then her eyes opened.

'Tell her, if you see her, that Sister Geneviève remembers her in her prayers.'

'I certainly will.' Seymour hesitated. 'She is in Naples. Shall I tell her that you would like to see her?'

Sister Geneviève's face lit up.

'Oh, yes!' she said. 'But tell her not to bother if it is difficult. Or if – if she doesn't want to.'

'I think she might want to,' said Seymour.

'You have to be,' said the Marchesa morosely, 'pretty desperate to go and look at boats.'

They had wandered down from the Porta del Carmine to the old harbour and then along to the Porto Mercantile, at this time of day crowded with fishing boats sighing against the quays. And there they had come across the Marchesa, sitting on a stone bollard with several iron rings in it, from which ropes led to various boats.

'And you are desperate, Marchesa?' asked Seymour.

'Desperately bored,' said the Marchesa. 'Naples is a pig of a place. Especially when the officers are doing whatever it is that officers spend their time doing. Manoeuvres, is it?'

'Not when they're in barracks.'

'Which they are most of the time. They keep them cooped up like chickens, and, in the end, like chickens they lose their virility. When they get out, they spend their time riding bicycles! Not terrorizing, and delighting, the female population, as they would have done in the old days. The country's going to pot,' said the Marchesa gloomily. 'Naples!' she said. 'Why I ever came here, I do not know. Or, at least, I do: my bastard husband sent me.'

'Was it not your choice, Marchesa?'

'Choice! What sort of choice do you have when you have no money and your bastard husband says: "Luisa, it's Naples for you. Naples, or nothing!"'

'I hope that at least the money's come through,' said Seymour.

'Oh, he's generous in that way,' said the Marchesa.

'Something you've just said, Marchesa, rather interested me. When was it you decided to change your name?'

'Change my name?'

'To Luisa.'

'When I became respectable,' said the Marchesa, with a ghost of a smile.

'And, of course, wished to put the "Esposito" behind you.'

'I *didn't* wish to put it behind me. I clung on to it as long as I could. But my husband's family made me get rid of it.'

'And the Margareta at the same time?'

'You have been *digging*!' cried the Marchesa delightedly. 'Oh, how exciting! At last something is happening in Naples. You have found out about the Hospital!'

'I am sorry if you wished to have kept it a secret.'

'Secret?' cried the Marchesa. 'Certainly not! Let me tell you, Esposito is a name to be proud of in Naples. It shows you have made it on your own. Without anybody helping you. No, no; I can assure you that when I began singing professionally it was a great draw. Especially in Naples. They were ecstatic. Margareta Esposita. They loved it. Someone from the back streets, like them. If I could do it, so could they. Secret? It was my big selling point. Of course, when I moved into the aristocracy, it was *not* such a selling point! And I thought, Margareta, you've made it. You can pull the ladder up now. Or, at any rate, stop continually referring to the ladder!'

'Was Esposita your professional name?' asked Chantale curiously.

'At first. *My* name. It was my name. And my voice. I wanted to tell people that. "It's me!" I wanted to say. "Little old me! From down at the bottom. But I'm not staying there, loves, I bloody am not." And people loved it. Even that bastard Alessandro loved it.

'Of course, he was an Esposito too. Although, like me, he changed his name when he was on his way to the top. "If

143

you'd met me earlier," I told him, "before we changed our names, we could have stuck to them." I meant, as a gesture of defiance. Of course, I realize now that what I should have said was, as a way of economizing. That would have appealed to him.

'But at the time it was because he thought he had found a fellow spirit. You know, someone from the depths, as he was. He came from the docks. Right here! Although that's not what I'm looking at the boats for. I used to sing here. From time to time. I would creep out of the Hospital when it all got too much for me, when I couldn't stand any more of the goody-goody atmosphere, and would come down here, and when I wanted some money for sweets I would sing to them. They were my people. I never forgot that and later, when I stood on the stage, it was to them I was singing and not to the bow ties and sparkling necklaces. I might be Luisa on the outside, but on the inside I was still Margareta.'

'And are you still Margareta?' asked Seymour.

'Even more.'

'There is someone who remembers you as Margareta. We were talking to her. She would like to see you again. Sister Geneviève.'

'Sister Geneviève? Is she still alive?'

'And would like to talk to you. If you could bear to.'

'Bear to?'

'She wouldn't want you to come if you don't want to.'

'Sister Geneviève?'

'If you would like to.'

The Marchesa considered, and then stood up.

'Yes,' she said. 'I think I would like to. I shall go now. Immediately.'

She started to go, and then stopped.

'How strange!' she said. 'That you should be the one to tell me! A policeman from England!'

'Stranger still,' said Seymour, 'what led me there.'

'What did lead you there?' asked the Marchesa.

'A betting slip,' said Seymour, 'in a dead man's pocket.'

The Marchesa looked at him levelly. 'Scampion's?'

Seymour nodded.

'How did it get there, Marchesa?'

'I gave it him.'

'*You* gave it him?'

'Yes. He asked for it. When I was about to throw it away. It was out of date, you see. Expired. But it had my number on it. My number at the Hospital. I always used that number when I betted. Because it was me. That number was me. I told him this. And he looked at me peculiarly and asked if he could have it. Of course, I said yes, although afterwards I was a little sorry – sorry that I had told him, and sorry that I had given him the ticket. I felt as if I had given part of myself away.'

She laughed to herself.

'Foolish!' she said. 'Foolish, I know. And sentimental.'

She shook her head.

'And sentimental on his part too.' She sighed. 'Poor little Scampion! I think he had the teeniest bit of a passion for me. A passionlet. Yes, that is better. English diplomatic officials do not have passions. They have passionlets. Baby passions.

'And what about English policemen, Signora?' she said to Chantale. 'Do they have passions? Or just passionlets?'

'Working up to it,' said Seymour.

'Ah, yes,' said the sailcloth-stitcher, 'you're the crazy man Alberto was talking about. The man looking for the Magic Number.'

'Not *the* Magic Number,' said Seymour. 'But *my* magic number. I'm nearly there. I just need a little bit to complete it.'

'That's always the hardest bit,' said the sailcloth-stitcher, sighing.

'I was so close!' said Seymour.

'Were you?' said the sailcloth-stitcher, interested.

'It was all there,' said Seymour, 'apart from one little bit.'

'Were you using the Smorfia?'

'Yes, I was.'

'I always find it very helpful.'

'It's tried and tested,' said Seymour.

Tried and tested and invariably wrong, he said to himself.

'Stick to it!' advised the sailcloth-stitcher. 'You can't do better.'

'I'm sure the Smorfia's all right,' said Seymour. 'It's just hitting on the thing it gives the number to that's the problem. The basic idea's good. What happened on that day. You know, the day the Englishman was killed.'

'I remember the day well,' said the sailcloth-stitcher encouragingly.

'You do?'

'It was the day my needle broke. Do you think that could be something to do with it?'

'I remember the day well,' said the pipe-maker. 'It was terrible. There was blood all over the place!'

'The Englishman –?'

'No, no. Our Nando, he fell over and hurt his knee. He made such a row that you'd have thought his leg had come off. "For God's sake, give that child something," I said to my wife. "A lump of sugar or something. The noise he's making is going right through my head."'

'Grandpa saw someone running!'

'He did?'

'That's right.'

'Did he get a good look at him?'

'Oh, yes.'

'Could he describe him?'

'Pretty well. It was Pietro, you see.'

'Pietro?'

'Gianni's boy. He lives in a *basso* at the other end of the street. When he heard what had happened, he came running up. Didn't want to miss anything, you see.'

* * *

And more of that ilk. Perhaps it had not been such a good idea after all.

He repaired to the snail restaurant. His friends commiserated.

'There's bound to be a lot of dross along with the gold,' said Ernesto.

'The trouble is, there hasn't been any gold yet,' said Seymour.

'Well, you couldn't expect it. Not just like that. You've got to persist. Dig around a bit.'

'Stick to it!' Alberto advised. 'One of these days, it will leap out at you.'

Seymour was beginning to wish he had not thought of this daft idea. He was halfway along the street now and getting nowhere. It wasn't, now, that they were unwilling to talk to him. On the contrary, they were only too willing. They remembered the day very well. But what they remembered was nothing to do with Scampion. It had happened at the end of the street, which in their terms was a long way away. The Porta del Carmine was another world. Scampion had belonged to that world, not that of the *bassi*, and they found it hard even to imagine him.

'Persist!' the carpenter enjoined him. 'One of these days, as you said, it will leap out at you!'

That was another daft thing that Seymour wished he had not said.

The carpenter looked back down the street.

'Oops!' he said. 'I've been expecting someone. And there he is. I'd better get back or my wife will have it in for me.'

He got up from the table.

The *acquaiolo* looked along the street too.

'Has the time come round again?' he said. 'Already?'

'It comes round a bit too quickly for my liking,' said the carpenter. 'Is it just that I'm getting old, or is he really coming round more often?'

'I'm sorry to say,' said the *acquaiolo*, 'that it's you getting old. He comes round every fortnight, as regular as clockwork. And the fortnight is just about up.'

'I suppose it's better that way,' said the carpenter. 'I

147

mean, if he came round every month it would always seem a lot when you had to find the money. This way makes it more manageable.'

He hurried off down the street back to his *basso*, where, indeed, his wife was waiting for him, arms akimbo.

'I'd better get back, too,' said the *acquaiolo*. 'He's working up the street and it'll be my turn in a minute or two.'

He set off back to his *basso*.

'And mine, too,' said the snail-shop owner, going to fidget beneath his boxes.

Later that afternoon Seymour and Chantale passed that way again. Ernesto was standing in his snail restaurant looking glum.

'Was it more this time?' asked Seymour.

Ernesto gave a start.

'More?' he said.

'What you have to pay them,' said Seymour.

Ernesto looked around him cautiously.

'A bit,' he said. 'But it's not so much that.'

'No?'

'No. It's Jacopo.'

'Which is Jacopo?'

'Three doors down. The basket-maker. He's not been doing so well lately and he couldn't find it.'

'The money?'

'That's right. What he had to pay.'

'Have they broken him up?'

'No, no. Not yet, at any rate. They've just said that they will. If he can't find it by next week. Well, he won't be able to. Business is bad for basket-makers, not just him. He'll have to get out.'

'Leave the *basso*?'

'That's right.'

'What will he do?'

'He's got a brother in Benevento. But his brother's not much better off than he is. Still, they won't touch him there. All the same, it's bad.'

148

'Hard on the family?'

'He's got five. And his wife's still sick from their last. This is no time to be moving. I'm just going to take a bowl of soup round there. Would you like to come?'

The *basso* looked more like a junk shop than a workshop. There were half-finished chairs in the street outside and worn baskets awaiting repair. There were piles of rushes and heaps of twigs scattered about over the floor. A clothes line ran along the front of the *basso* and on it were various items of worn clothing together with stained pieces of cloth. A broken-down table stood outside and at it a man was working. The doors of the *basso* were only half open but inside he could just about make out in the darkness the large bed, on which children were playing. He couldn't see the mother but guessed she was in it.

Ernesto put the bowl on the table.

'For the little ones,' he said.

The man at the table looked up.

'Thank you, Ernesto. I will repay,' he said.

'Of course, you will, Jacopo,' said Ernesto heartily. 'When things are better, yes?'

The man shrugged.

'If they ever get better,' he said.

He gave a shout and two of the bigger children came out and eyed the bowl greedily.

'Take it to your mother; and see that she gets some of it.'

The children nodded and took the bowl away.

The man looked at Ernesto.

'He came again this morning,' he said.

'He came to me, too,' said Ernesto.

'I did them a favour a few weeks ago,' the man said. 'I thought that would be enough. For the time being. But he said it was only a little favour, and was only worth two payments. And I'd had those.'

'Was the favour worth more?' asked Seymour.

The man shrugged.

'Perhaps not,' he said. 'But it was worth trying.'

149

'Perhaps they could make it worth three payments?' suggested Ernesto. 'If you ask them?'

The man shrugged and didn't say anything.

'What was the favour you did for them?' asked Seymour.

'It was nothing,' the man said. 'That's the trouble. I just looked the other way.'

'When the man stepped into the *basso*?' said Seymour.

'Yes,' said the basket-maker, surprised. 'That's right.'

'Important to him,' said Seymour. 'But perhaps not to them.'

'It was important to him at the time,' said the basket-maker bitterly.

'And so it should have been to them,' said Seymour.

'Suggest it's worth three payments,' urged Ernesto. 'Perhaps they will think again.'

'Perhaps,' said the basket-maker. He seemed unconvinced.

The children came out again with the empty bowl and gave it back to Ernesto. Then they drew themselves up in a line formally.

'We thank you, Ernesto.'

'It is nothing, it is nothing,' said Ernesto.

'Our mother says you are a good man, Ernesto.'

'Not good enough,' said Ernesto.

Chapter Eleven

Seymour went out into the streets around the Porta del Carmine and at last he found what he was looking for. The open doors of a *basso* extended across the street and he stood in the partition they made, behind a row of washing, and watched the man work his way up the street. Then he went back to the *pensione*.

Maria was putting out the dishes for the evening meal: a heavy white plate and then a bowl on it for the soup.

'I have just made some coffee?' she said.

'Please.'

He sat down at a table in the corner and waited. When she brought the coffee he thanked her and then said quietly:

'Did they call here, too?'

'Call?' she said, startled.

'The people whose name we don't mention.'

Maria said nothing but continued to put out the plates.

'I have seen them collecting in other streets,' said Seymour.

'They collect here, too,' said Maria.

'From you?'

Maria shook her head fiercely.

'Not from us,' she said. 'From us, never!'

'But they have tried?'

'Oh, yes, they have tried. Once they came with a gun. But Giuseppi went into the bedroom and came back with *his* gun. It was the one he had used on the barricades, but that was when he was a young man and he has not used

151

it since. There was a time when he kept it clean but he hasn't done that for twenty years. If he fired it, it would probably blow *him* up. But they were not to know that, and ran away.'

'And haven't come back?'

'They know Giuseppi and respect him. They know that in the quarter he is admired, as a man of the barricades. They know it is best not to touch people like that.'

'And yet you allow them into your house,' said Seymour quietly.

'I?' said Maria.

'Bruno,' said Seymour. 'He is a collector, isn't he? Jalila said he was, and I have just been watching him at work.'

'We have known Bruno for a long time,' said Maria. 'His mother and I were delivered in the same week. In the same street. We have stayed close since. Our boys played together, Marcello and Bruno . . . Bruno has been in and out of the house ever since he could walk. He has been a good son to his mother. When his father died, that very day he went out to find work. He knew he had to.'

'And he found collecting?' said Seymour.

'Not at first. He did other jobs. But he was young, and he was small, and he couldn't do the heavy jobs, like lifting barrels. But they knew he was a sturdy boy and, I suppose, they knew his need.'

Maria shrugged and wiped the table.

'A man has to earn a living,' she said. 'All of us. And sometimes it may not be in the way we would like.'

'Is it the way you would like for Jalila's husband?'

'That is for Jalila herself to say.'

'And what does Jalila say?'

'She wonders. Bruno thinks he is doing right by Tonio.' She shrugged again. 'I don't know if that is true. If our Marcello were here, I would ask him. He would probably agree with Bruno.'

'The three of them, Bruno, Tonio and your Marcello, were close, weren't they?' said Seymour.

'As close as that,' said Maria, holding her fingers

together in the manner that Chantale said Bruno had when he was talking to her.

'And does Jalila wish it?'

'To marry Bruno? She doesn't know what she wishes.'

'He has money.'

'While he does what they ask, he has money.'

'I can understand her doubts,' said Seymour.

'He would be a good husband to her, as he has been a good son to his mother. And she would be a good daughter to his mother. That is important, as his mother is old now and has not been well for some time.'

'And the children? Would he be a good father to them?'

Maria thought.

'He would not be a bad father,' she said. 'He is kind, although not always patient. I do not know.' She shrugged. 'Who does know what a man will be like when be becomes a father? And when the children are not his? I do not know. But this I know: any father is better than no father.'

Giorgio appeared in the doorway.

'Hello, Maria! Is Francesca inside?'

'She is. But she still has work to do.'

'What sort of work?'

'Sweeping the floors.'

'Perhaps I can help her,' said Giorgio, disappearing inside.

'Will he do that?' asked Seymour. 'When he gets older?'

Maria considered.

'Most of them go and hang about in the piazza,' she said, 'and leave their wives to do everything in the house.'

'I am not sure that Francesca would be content with that,' said Seymour.

'I am not sure, either. In the first flush, perhaps. But after? I wonder.'

She rubbed the table.

'Francesca deserves better things,' she said.

Francesca came into the room.

'Have you any small change?' she asked. 'Jalila wants to send a letter and they have only given her big notes.'

'Look in my purse,' directed Maria. 'How much does she want? If it is to send a letter to Libya – I expect she wants to tell her people about the pension,' she said to Seymour – 'then it will be a lot.'

'No, it's to Rome,' said Francesca.

'I didn't think she knew anybody in Rome,' said Maria.

Francesca inspected the letter she had been given.

'No, it's definitely Rome,' she said. 'It is addressed to someone at a bank.'

Seymour went upstairs to find Chantale. They had arranged to go out for dinner that evening and she was changing her dress.

When they came down they found Jalila standing uncertainly in the door of the kitchen.

'Maria has forgotten to take her purse with her,' she said. 'She has gone out to do some shopping and she will need it.'

'Do you know which way she went?' asked Chantale.

'I think she will have gone to the baker's,' said Jalila. 'It's just round the corner and I can catch up with her if I run.'

She hesitated, and then said to Chantale, gesturing at the children: 'Would you mind? Just for a moment?'

'Of course not!' said Chantale, slipping her hand into the hand of the little boy. 'Shall we go out on to the patio?'

'Thank you,' said Jalila gratefully. 'I won't be a moment. I think Maria had been putting some money in her purse and then someone called for her and she put it down.'

She sped off.

'I don't want to go on to the patio,' said the child.

'Where do you want to go? We cannot go far, because your mummy will be back in a minute, and we don't want to miss her.'

'He wants to go to the sweet shop,' said the boy's sister.

'Well, I don't know about that . . .' said Chantale. 'We'll see what your mother says. We can go and look in the window if you like. Then you can make up your mind and we'll see what your mother thinks when she gets back.'

154

They trooped along the street, the little boy holding happily to Chantale's hand, his older sister in earnest conversation with Seymour.

Miss Scampion came round the corner pushing her bicycle.

'Good heavens!' she said. 'Where did you get these from?'

'They're Jalila's children,' said Chantale. 'You know, the Libyan lady you sometimes see around here.'

'Libyan, yes,' said Miss Scampion. 'You can see the Arab.'

'And the Italian,' said Seymour.

'And the Italian, of course,' said Miss Scampion. 'So that is their mother? Jalila?'

'Yes, we are minding the children just for the moment.'

'Kind of you, yes. And – Jalila is the name of their mother?'

'Yes. She lives nearby. With her parents-in-law. She is a widow. Her husband was killed in the war. So one could say that this is a military family, too.'

'Ah, yes, but it is not quite the same, is it, my dear? He would have been just a trooper.'

'Troopers get killed, too,' said Chantale.

Miss Scampion was not, however, listening.

'Jalila,' she said meditatively. 'Lionel spoke about her.'

'Did he?' said Seymour, surprised.

'I am almost sure Jalila was the name.'

'I wonder how he ran into her?'

'I think he knew someone in Florence. Or was it Rome? I think it might have been Rome. Anyway, this person, a diplomatic acquaintance of Lionel's, I believe, was trying to do something for her. In her plight, you know. Somehow he had become acquainted with her and wanted to help her. He *had* helped her, I believe. Anyway, he knew that Lionel was being transferred to Naples and asked him to look her up.

'I had my doubts about this, I must confess. How could he be expected to find her? A woman new in Naples. And then what could he do for her when he found her? It was all very well for his friend, a rich man, I believe, to say: look her up. But in the Diplomatic, you know, you move in fairly restricted social circles. And they do not include the wives of troopers.'

'Perhaps Mr Scampion's acquaintance gave him an address?' said Seymour.

'Perhaps. Yes, almost certainly. But then, what was Lionel supposed to do for her? See that she was all right for money? But, you know, although Lionel was always most generous, he did not have money to give. The two of us were scrimping and saving, especially after the move to Naples. Fitting out a new house costs money, and I do not think the people in London quite recognize that. There is an allowance, of course, but no one would call it generous. It was all very well for Lionel's friend to ask him to look after her, but he was a rich man.'

'Perhaps he gave Mr Scampion some money to pass on to her?' said Seymour.

'Perhaps. I hope so. I was afraid that Lionel might be tempted.'

'To give her money?'

'That, too, yes. But . . .' She hesitated. 'I feared that he might be tempted in another way, too. If she engaged his sympathies. And Lionel's sympathies were easily engaged, you know. All too easily. That dreadful Marchesa! And I feel that a woman alone might well engage his sympathies. More than they should. Lionel was always very susceptible, you know.'

Miss Scampion dropped her voice. 'It runs in the family. On the male side. There was a cousin of his – oh, I don't like to speak about it. Cashiered. And even Uncle was not immune. You can understand it, I suppose. Soldiers are men, after all. As I am sure you found, Miss de Lissac. And in a lonely outpost –'

'I am not sure that Naples counts as a lonely outpost, Miss Scampion,' said Seymour.

'No, no, of course not. But is it not nearly the same thing, Mr Seymour? If not a lonely outpost, a lonely man. In

156

whom passions – well, rise. And then perhaps his work – or, as in Lionel's case, the request of a friend – brings him perforce into contact with a lady who is not entirely –'

'I don't think that is the case here, Miss Scampion,' said Seymour. 'I feel I must speak in defence of your brother. And the lady in question. She has always seemed most scrupulous to me.'

'Oh, yes, I am sure, I am sure. But, you see, it was more than once. It was, in fact, *quite often.*'

'What was, Miss Scampion?'

'His going to see her. Once I could understand. At the request of a friend. Especially if it was to give her something. Like money. But he met her several times, Mr Seymour, and he could not *always* have been giving her money, could he? Or, at least – well, no. No, I am sure!'

'He may have felt she needed support,' said Seymour.

'Oh, yes, indeed! And Lionel was always more than generous with his support. He could always be relied upon to give a helping hand. And that might have been how it started. But could it not have led on, Mr Seymour, to something more?'

'I don't see why you should suppose that, Miss Scampion.'

She was silent for a moment. Then she said: 'Once I saw them. They were talking together more intimately. I had always imagined that he called on her at her residence. But, no, this was in a public park. Among the trees. I was on my bicycle taking the air. And I saw them.

'When he got home, I tackled him about it. "It's a lady I am helping," he said. "Well, that's very nice of you, Lionel," I said. "But do you have to help her in such an intimate fashion?"

'He went red, and I knew he was angry. But this was at the time when he always seemed to be angry and I felt that I had had enough of his deception. "Is this what has been making you so angry?" I said. "A guilty conscience?"

'He just looked at me. "No," he said, "not a guilty conscience. At least, not over this. Not over something I have done, but over something I haven't done and ought to have done."

"'Is it to do with that woman?" I demanded. "No," he said. "At least, not directly. All she has done is help me see things in perspective." "I cannot believe that, Lionel," I said. "For lately you do *not* seem to have been seeing things in perspective. You have always seemed so angry." "Over some things," he said, "anger is the only right response."'

Late that afternoon, when the heat was beginning to lift from the streets and the piazzas to fill with people taking the air, Chantale went out by herself to buy something. She arranged to meet Seymour at the Capuana Gate.

When he arrived she hailed him with relief. Vincente, she complained, was following her around 'like a little dog'.

She had run into him in a shop and then not been able to shake him off. He had offered to carry her shopping for her. How much he thought she would be buying, she couldn't imagine. She suspected that, used to performing a similar function for the Marchesa, his estimates were large. Chantale's shopping, however, was governed by her purse, and that was small. She didn't need a carrier, and she certainly didn't need someone going round behind her droopily all the time.

Except, possibly, Seymour. However, going shopping with him was usually a dead loss. He was so plainly un-interested in *any* shopping that it put her off. Usually she sent him away after the first few minutes.

Today, however, she would have been glad of him, for Vincente was worse. At least Seymour could be relied on to confirm the shrewdness of her shopping. Admittedly, in the field of shopping, at any rate, he tended to confirm all her judgements and she was slightly suspicious about this; but Vincente didn't seem able to rise to even that level. He just followed her around with blank, dog-like eyes of devotion, and it got on her nerves.

158

How the hell he would manage in the army in Libya she couldn't think. Perhaps that was what everyone else thought, too. Certainly the Marchesa, who, for all her faults, seemed to be a sharp judge of people. Perhaps that was why she refused to let him go out there? Got her husband, who seemed able to pull plenty of strings, to intervene?

A sharp judge, but possibly a soft heart? She seemed to have taken Scampion's measure; but hadn't she intervened when he had proposed to volunteer for Libya? From all that Chantale had heard, she had been completely right about that.

'Ah!' said Chantale, now brightly. 'Here is my fiancé!'

And waited.

But Vincente did not go.

'We're just about to go back to the *pensione*,' said Chantale firmly.

'Are we?' said Seymour, puzzled.

Really, he was rather obtuse at times, thought Chantale.

'Yes,' she said firmly; and took her fiancé by the arm and started off.

Vincente followed.

And, what was worse, Seymour started talking to him!

'I expect you're very busy just at the moment. With the race coming off at the weekend.'

'Oh, I am, I am!'

'But then I expect you always are. Handling things on the bicycle side, I mean.'

'Well, that's true.'

'There are always problems, I expect.'

'Well . . .'

'Like that package a few weeks ago.'

'Package?'

'Of bicycle parts. Fortunately, Signor Scampion spotted it in time.'

'Oh, yes. That package. He got very excited about it. Said I ought to do something. They had been misdirected, you see. They weren't meant for us at all. "Does it matter?" I said. "Yes," he said. "It matters a lot!" And he kept on at me. Saying I ought to do something. He seemed quite angry. I was puzzled, because – well – it didn't seem that important. "Stores are always doing that kind of thing," I said. "Oh, are they?" he said. "Then that's all the more reason to do something about it."

'He went on and on and in the end I thought I *had* better do something about it. Of course, I'm not Stores but I am, in a way, Bicycles, and this was bicycles, so I sent a message back to the factory.

'And the next moment all hell broke loose. There was my cousin, Alessandro, on the phone to me, saying what the hell did I think I was doing? What did I know about it? "Nothing," I said hastily. "Nothing!" "Then shut up!" he said. "Or the next time you really will go to Libya." So I shut up.

'Next week, the package had gone. That's good, I said to myself. They've done something about it. Taken it back in for checking. But then I learned that it had been sent on to Libya!

'They've cocked it up *again*, I thought. And I rang the factory and told them so. And then Alessandro came down on me again like a ton of bricks. This time he was *really* cross. "Haven't you got any sense at all?" he demanded. He was really unpleasantly rude. I complained to Luisa. "Just forget about it," she said. "I always do when it's Alessandro." "Yes, but he's been really rude!" I said. "Very probably," she said, "knowing my husband.

'"But, darling, aren't you being just the tiniest bit dumb? This is obviously something you're meant to keep out of. It's over your head. I know, sweetie, that most things are, and on the whole it doesn't matter. But if Alessandro is anything to do with it, it *does* matter. So keep out of it, dumbo. You've had the warning. Now just keep out of it."

'So I did. But Scampion kept on at me. And in the end I told him there was no longer anything I could do about it, it had been sent on to Libya. "Jesus!" he cried. "But that's Arabs! They're your enemy!"

'"I don't see anything wrong with them getting bicycle parts," I said. "Enemy or no. I mean, it might do some good. If they're all bicycling and not fighting. Better bicycle than shoot, especially when they might be shooting us."

'"But these are *not* bicycle parts!" he cried.

'"Well, if they've got it wrong again, that's their look-out," I said. "I'm sorry about them not being able to bicycle, but I've done what I can."

'"For Christ's sake!" he said. "Can't you understand? These are *not* bicycle parts."

'"Well, are you sure?" I said. "I've seen the labelling, and they definitely came from Dion."

'"But Dion makes other things besides bicycles!" he said.

'"I'm sure they do," I said. "But, look –"

'But he had gone off in a fury.'

'And then another consignment arrived. I was going to do nothing about it but Scampion was on the lookout and he saw it.

'"It's still going on!" he cried. "This is wrong! This is immoral!"

'He seemed to me to be making a fuss about nothing, so I just tut-tutted, and shook my head, and said "Dear, dear!"

'"This time you really have got to do something," he said.

'"I could go direct to Alessandro, I suppose," I said, rather doubtfully.

'"A waste of time," he said. "I'm going to go to the Ministry."

'"I know I'm not very bright," I said, "and I don't know much about these things, or, indeed, about anything: but I do know this. That really *would* be a waste of time!"

'He looked at me thoughtfully. "You're probably right," he said.

'"They're sure to be in Dion's pocket," I said.

'"Maybe I'd better go to the newspapers," he said.

'"They'll be in Dion's pocket, too," I said.

'"Not all of them," he said. "Not all of them."

'I suddenly knew what he was thinking. There are two camps, you see, in the bicycle world. Dion's – he publishes

161

Auto-Vélo – and Gifford's – he publishes *Vélo*. And they're deadly rivals. I knew that what Scampion was thinking of was going to the *Vélo*. It would publish anything bad about Dion.

'Well, the more I thought about this, the less I liked the sound of it. I thought it might come back on us, and on me especially, because I was the one who had raised the questions about the package in the first place. I thought and thought and in the end I decided the best thing I could do was go straight to Alessandro and make a clean breast of it. It would be awful, I knew. He would be *really* unpleasant to me. But at least it would be over and done with. And, besides, I told myself, he would certainly find out about it anyway, and he already knew my connection with it. So I went to Alessandro.

'But, of course, I didn't want to land Scampion in it so I didn't tell him about Scampion at all. I just said that a little bird had told me that something about the package might be about to appear in the *Vélo*.

'Of course, he was on to me in a flash. "How do you know about this?" he asked. "A little bird told me," I said. Well, he pressed me and pressed me – really bullied me, it was most unpleasant. But I stuck to my guns. "I've just heard it," I said.

'He wouldn't give up. "You're sure you don't know the name of this little bird, Vincente?" he said.

'But I stood firm. "I'm sure I don't know it," I said.

'"You see, Vincente," he said, "this is Italy, and in Italy little birds get caught in a net, and then they have their necks wrung."

'The way he said it made me feel quite cold. But I didn't give way. "If I knew the name, I wouldn't tell you," I said.

'He just sat there and looked at me. For quite a long time. And then he smiled. "Well, thanks for telling me, anyway," he said. "I won't forget this, Vincente. You're a good boy, and I think you could go far. Just come and talk to me whenever you're in trouble. I'll see you're all right. You're a cousin, after all, and blood is thicker than water. I promised your mother that I would look after you and I will. So don't worry. I'll take care of this. The only thing is this, and this I absolutely insist on, you mustn't say anything about this to anyone. You see, there are commercial interests involved, and not just mine, I must say. If anything got out it could do a lot of damage. And that would have repercussions. They're a cut-throat lot, you see, businessmen, and have to be handled with care. So just keep quiet about all this, will you, Vincente? There's a good fellow."

'"I certainly will," I said. "The less I have to do with business, the better."

'"Quite right, my boy. Quite right. Leave it to the experts," he said.

'"Although I have to say that they cannot be that expert," I said. "To get a simple matter like sending a package wrong!"

'"Well, there you are!" sighed Alessandro.

'"Especially when it's something really important. Like bicycle parts."

'"Bicycle parts?" said Alessandro. He seemed quite lost for the moment. Then – "Bicycle parts," he said thoughtfully. And smiled.'

Chapter Twelve

Suddenly, that evening, the *pensione* became for some reason very agitated. Maria and Giuseppi went around with perturbed faces and even Francesca was untypically subdued.

In the kitchen Maria and Giuseppi were talking in low voices.

'I *told* you!' Maria said. 'I *told* you to have nothing to do with them.'

'I've *had* nothing to do with them!'

'Yes, you have!'

'Not directly,' Giuseppi qualified.

'It amounts to the same thing.'

'Look, how was I to know? It seemed a good idea at the time.'

'You shouldn't have involved them.'

'We didn't really involve them. It was just that Rinaldo thought it would clinch it.'

'Mentioning their name?'

'Yes. They were being a bit slow in the office, you know, and –'

'You fools!' said Maria passionately.

'It might never have come through otherwise. You know what they are –'

'And I know what Our Friends are. How could you do it, Giuseppi? How could you do it?'

'Look, you wanted it for her, didn't you? You told me to get down to the office. You even suggested – yes, you're the one who suggested it – taking Rinaldo and Pietro.'

'I thought it would lend weight.'

'It did, it did!'

'But not enough, evidently! You had to try and lend it more!'

'It was Rinaldo's idea,' said Giuseppi feebly.

'To use their name?'

'Well, it wasn't exactly using their name –'

'Oh, wasn't it? What do you think got the office moving then?'

'It was a sort of casual reference. And Rinaldo went along afterwards to make it right with them.'

'Well, he doesn't seem to have succeeded, does he?'

'I don't understand it. He doesn't understand it. It seemed all right. They didn't make anything of it – at the time.'

'Well, they have now, haven't they?'

Rinaldo had come along earlier in the evening, very much perturbed, even shaken. He had gone straight into the kitchen and had remained closeted there with Maria and Giuseppi for quite some time. Francesca had had to serve the meal on her own and she had done it with tight lips and a pale face.

Rinaldo had just left, hurriedly, and with head bowed.

'Giuseppi, what have you done?'

'I can't understand it! It seemed all right!'

'And now it's not all right!'

'Something has changed. It must have! This sort of thing is nothing to them. A pension for someone? They're doing it all the time. And for the widow of an Italian soldier? There's usually no bother. They're glad to do it. It makes them look good. Why is there this sudden change?'

'Could it be that she's an Arab?' said Maria.

'Well, that sort of thing doesn't normally bother them. It's enough that she's the widow of an Italian soldier from Naples –'

'It's enough for you, Giuseppi. But is it enough for them?'

'It *was* enough. Christ, if it hadn't been, they would have said something at the time.'

Maria was silent. Then she said: 'You're probably right.

Something has changed. Since Rinaldo spoke to them. And I wonder what it can be?' she said thoughtfully.

'They've got it in for Jalila,' said Giuseppi.

'They've got it in for *us*. That's what's worrying me,' said Maria.

'If they try anything on me, I'll shoot their balls off,' said Giuseppi. 'I've still got my gun.'

'Your gun is even older than you are, Giuseppi. Don't be foolish!'

'I'm not giving in. I've seen others give in. It gets you nowhere.'

'Jalila will have to leave,' said Maria, with decision.

'Where can she go to?'

'We'll find somewhere. I've got a cousin up in the mountains. She'll be out of the way there.'

'We ought to speak to Bruno. Where the hell *is* Bruno?'

Where the hell *was* Bruno? Giorgio was sent out to find him. He was not at home and not on any of his usual beats. His mother said he had gone to Rome.

But, then, his mother's mind was a little askew these days. And was it likely? To the best of everyone's knowledge Bruno had rarely set foot outside Naples. And what would have led him to take such a step now, suddenly, and without telling anyone? It seemed unlikely.

But then came a report that Bruno had been seen near the railway station the day before.

This, however, was not conclusive. For if Bruno had rarely set foot outside Naples before, even more rarely had he ever stepped into a train. Like many decent Neapolitans, and all poor Neapolitans, he had a distrust for the new, and that still included trains.

And, again, was it likely?

But if he had not left the city, then where was he?

As time went by there was an increasing foreboding that he was where people who disappeared in Naples usually were: in some back alley, dead.

* * *

But the probability of this, too, seemed less after something that happened later on in the evening. Seymour and Chantale were sitting out on the patio in the soft, warm darkness of the Italian evening – it was still too hot to go indoors – when there was an eruption of noise at the front of the *pensione*. Voices were raised.

'Why come to me?' said Giuseppi.

'Don't answer us back. Just tell us where he is!' said a rough voice.

'You're more likely to know that than we are,' said Giuseppi.

'We don't know,' said Maria less belligerently.

'No?' said the man threateningly.

'No,' said Giuseppi. 'And if we did, we wouldn't tell you.'

Seymour got up and went to the door. Not for the first time he wished he had a gun, but he hadn't. The police in London never carried guns and he certainly wasn't carrying one now.

'Don't push your luck, old man!' said the man warningly.

'And don't push yours,' retorted Giuseppi. 'I've met your sort before.'

'Oh, we know all about you on the barricades!' sneered the man.

'Well, you weren't on them, that's for sure!' said Giuseppi sturdily.

'I wasn't born then!'

'Leave it!' commanded a fresh voice. 'We've no quarrel with you, old man. Just tell us where Bruno is.'

'We don't know,' said Maria. 'That's the truth of it. We haven't seen him for a day or two. We've been looking for him. Some say he's gone to Rome.'

'Yes, we've heard that, too,' said the man who seemed to be their leader.

'Is he with that Arab bitch?' demanded the other man.

'I don't know anyone of that description,' said Maria coldly.

'If you're talking about the widow of an Italian soldier –' began Giuseppi.

'Yes, yes, we know all about that, too. Tonio's wife,' said the leader impatiently.

'Is Bruno with her?' demanded the other man.

'Not as far as we know. He's not with her that often.'

'No?'

'No. He's much more likely to be with his mother, and don't you go bothering her!' said Maria hastily. 'She's an old lady and frail.'

'We just want to know where he is,' said the leader.

'Why?' said Maria.

'We want to talk to him. That's all. We don't intend him any harm. In fact,' he said, 'we want to offer him a job.'

The other man laughed.

'That's right,' he said.

'You must have plenty of other people you could get to do it,' said Maria.

'Oh, yes, but this is a special job. And we think it's one for Bruno to do.'

The other man laughed again.

'That's right,' he agreed. 'One for him.'

'Well, we don't know where he is,' said Maria. 'And he's certainly not with Jalila, so you can leave her alone.'

'Try Rome,' said Giuseppi. 'And you can go there on a bicycle as far as I'm concerned.'

The leader laughed.

'You've still got plenty of spirit, old man. I like that. Just don't let it carry you too far, that's all. Look after him, Mother,' he said to Maria. 'Keep him out of this.'

'That's just what I've been trying to do,' said Maria.

'Come on,' the man said to the men with him. There appeared to be at least two of them. 'Let's go! And if you see Bruno,' he said to Maria, 'tell him we want to see him. Tell him it's all right. He's got nothing to worry about. It's just that we want to see him and talk to him.'

'And offer him a job,' said one of the other men, laughing.

They went out of the other door. Seymour was glad it had not come to anything. If it had, he would have felt obliged to step in, and he didn't fancy his chances against three of them. They were probably armed, too. In the East End it would very likely have been enough just to show himself. The presence of a policeman, or even just of a witness, was usually enough to do the trick. Here he was not quite so sure.

'I wonder if he really has gone to Rome?' the leader was saying, as he went through the door. 'What the hell would he want to go there for?'

The problem – or at least the problem of Bruno's disappearance – seemed to have been resolved the next day, for Bruno reappeared.

'Where have you been, Bruno?' cried Francesca. 'Everyone's been looking for you.'

'Rome,' said Bruno shortly. 'I need to talk to Maria. Where is she?'

'Making the beds,' said Francesca. 'I'll go and fetch her.'

Bruno stood fidgeting in the doorway. He replied to Seymour's greeting politely but briefly.

'Is Giuseppi around?' he asked Giorgio, who was polishing shoes. This appeared to be another of his jobs.

'He's around somewhere,' said Giorgio. 'Do you want me to go and look for him?'

'Maria's the one I want to see.'

Giorgio returned to his polishing.

'What's Rome like?' he asked curiously.

'Big,' said Bruno. 'And everyone's rushing. It's not like Naples.'

'They say that Rome is where it all happens.'

Bruno gave a short laugh.

'They may be right,' he said.

'You didn't stay long,' said Giorgio, after a moment.

'Long enough,' said Bruno.

Giorgio waited, but he didn't say any more. Giorgio shrugged and got on with his polishing.

Maria came down the stairs at that moment.

'Why, Bruno,' she said, with some relief, 'it is good to see you.'

'I need to talk to you, Maria,' he said.

'Come in.'

She led him into the kitchen and shut the door. This was unusual. Doors in the *pensione* were usually left open to create a through draught. Francesca, however, carrying things to and fro, opened it a little later and Seymour heard the tail-end of the conversation inside.

'You'll see to it, then,' said Bruno.

'I'll write to my cousin today,' Maria promised.

'That's no good,' said Bruno. 'It will take too long. You've got to get her out of here *immediately*.'

'I'll send her to Simone. She's at San Sebastian. You know, where Father Pepe used to live. Then she can go from there to my cousin.'

'It will be all right, will it?' said Bruno. 'We don't want anyone talking, and you know what they are in a village.'

'I'll get Pepe to take her over there and he can talk to them. They'll listen to him.'

'It would be better if no one knew about it.'

'I'll say that to Pepe too. He's an intelligent man.'

'Right, then,' said Bruno, and came to the door.

'You'll be all right yourself, Bruno?' said Maria anxiously. 'You know what they are.'

'I will be all right,' said Bruno.

'They'll know you've been to Rome.'

'I'll tell them I went to see a woman,' said Bruno.

'It's a long way to go to see a woman. They'll wonder.'

'I'll work out a story.'

'Just be careful, that's all. They came here looking for you, you know.'

'For me?' said Bruno. 'Or for her?'

'For you first. Then they thought you might be with her.'

'Bastards!' said Bruno.

'Just be careful, that's all.'

'I'll be careful.'

Maria came to the door with him.

'It may be all right,'she said. 'They told me to tell you that you were not to worry. It was just they had a job for you.'

'A job for me?' Bruno laughed bitterly. 'I can guess what that job is. That's why I went to Rome.'

As Seymour and Chantale were going along a back street, full of *bassi* and children, there came suddenly a strong smell of goats. A herd appeared around a corner, filling the street completely and blocking the way. A woman leaned out of a window above and shouted. The man with the goats said something and the lead goat stopped. It probably would have done so anyway on hearing the woman's voice. The herd stopped too.

'A moment, Signora,' said the man.

The woman let fall a small pail on a rope. The man caught it and took it over to one of the goats. Then he bent down beside it and milked it into the pail. Then he took the pail and tied it to the rope again and the woman hauled it up.

'How much?' she called.

The man said something but his dialect was so rough that Seymour could not understand him. The woman could, however, and put some coins in the pail and lowered it again.

'At least it stays the same!' she called down.

'Everything in Naples stays the same!' said the man, and this time Seymour could understand him.

The herd parted and let Seymour and Chantale through and then continued on its way.

The woman leaned out of the window again and started a conversation with a woman on the other side of the street who was hanging out some washing. She appeared to have some arrangement with a house on the other side for a clothes line stretched between the houses. The woman pulled it in, pegged out her washing, and then ran it out again so that the washing hung out over the street. There were men's drawers, a woman's petticoat, and a string of nappies.

'Babies!' said a voice. 'In Naples. Always babies!'

It was the Marchesa, on one of her lonely patrols.

'And what about you, Signora?' she said to Chantale. 'Have you thought about making babies yet?'

'Not really,' said Chantale, startled.

'There's time enough,' said the Marchesa. 'For you, if not for me.' She glanced up at the clothes line overhead. 'And, looking at that lot,' she said, 'I don't know whether to be glad or sorry!'

She shook her head. 'But it wouldn't do,' she said, 'not for a singer. Babies and a career don't go together. However,' she said firmly, 'money does.'

'And that was your choice?' said Chantale.

The Marchesa shrugged.

'I had no choice,' she said. 'Not if I wished to get out of the world the Foundling Hospital condemned me to.'

'With hindsight,' said Seymour, 'looking back now: which man, no doubt of many, if things had been different, would you have chosen to have children by?'

The Marchesa laughed delightedly.

'Well, there's a thought!' she said.

She considered. 'D'Annunzio? No. As a lover, fine; as a father . . .'

She shook her head. 'No, I really think not. He would have been hopeless. And what an example!'

She thought some more. 'Roberto? My first husband? No, not really. He gave me the title but there was not much chance of him giving me anything else. The line was pretty exhausted by the time it got to Roberto. No chance, I would say.'

She thought again.

'You know, this could go on for a long time,' she said.

'Alessandro?'

'Alessandro? Hmm. He would clearly have loved it, of course. Indeed, he suggested it. "But haven't we left it a bit late?" I said. "A few years ago, perhaps." But, you know, even then . . .'

172

She shook her head. '"Why add to the bastards already in the world?" I said to him. "A son might turn out like you." That angered him. "Or a daughter?" he said. "Mightn't she turn out like you?"

'I have to admit that was a consideration. I wouldn't wish a fate like that on any poor girl.'

She shook her head again. 'So Alessandro, no. On reflection, definitely no. So who then? Surely among the many men I have known there must be somebody? Of course, my standards are high. Speaking theoretically, that is.'

She gave a little, delightful laugh.

'You know,' she said, 'I think in the end it would probably come down to that little Englishman.'

'Scampion?'

'Yes.'

'The one you gave the lottery slip to?'

'You should have seen his face when I gave it him. It was as if I had given him – well, let's say myself. He would have given me pure devotion. Well, that's something you don't come across very often, and I certainly never have. Not pure.

'But the thing is, he would have offered that to our children as well, and that's what you want. That's something Alessandro would never have been capable of. He would have loved them, yes: but possessively, greedily, jealously. But disinterestedly? For themselves alone? I think not. They would just have been an extension of him. The poor little buggers would never have had a life of their own. And suppose one of them had been like me? Always kicking against the pricks. And that, of course, brings me back to Alessandro . . .

'No, Lionel – a misnomer of a name if there ever was one – wouldn't have been like that. He would have been a proper father. Such as I never had.

'And, just think about it,' she continued, though, excitedly: 'I could have left them with him while I went out and got on with my life. Safe in the knowledge that I was behaving responsibly. Because certainly they would have

173

been better off with him than they would have been with me. No, little Scampion it is. Definitely.'

On an impulse, Seymour said: 'Would you like to meet some admirers of yours?'

'Not much,' said the Marchesa.

'They go back a long time. To the time when you first started singing opera in Naples.'

'Ah, well, that's different.'

He took her to the snail restaurant.

'I wonder what they're like now,' she said, almost wistfully.

'Would you like to try some?'

'Why not?' said the Marchesa.

The carpenter and the *acquaiolo* were sitting at the table. They looked up, stared, and then jumped to their feet.

Ernesto reeled, then recovered.

'You honour me,' he said, 'Margareta.'

'Margareta!' said the Marchesa. She smiled. 'So I am not entirely forgotten, then?'

'You will never be forgotten!' said the snail-shop owner, fervently.

The carpenter was still staring.

'This cannot be true!' he said.

'He said he had seen you,' said the *acquaiolo*, 'but I did not believe him!'

'You have come back to us, Margareta,' said Ernesto.

'I should never have left,' said the Marchesa.

'It was only right that you should take your talent to the world!' declared the carpenter.

'The world!' said the Marchesa. She shrugged. 'The world is not that special a place.'

'But your voice,' said the *acquaiolo*, 'that is special!'

'No longer,' said the Marchesa. 'It grows old, as we all grow old.'

'Oh, no!' they all cried in unison. 'You will never grow old, Margareta. Not in our hearts.'

174

'Thank you!'

She laughed. 'But even hearts grow old.'

She sniffed. 'But do the snails grow old?'

She sniffed again. 'Can I try some?'

Ernesto, hand shaking, ladled some into a bowl and then watched anxiously.

The Marchesa tasted, reflected, and then tasted again.

'They do not grow old,' she pronounced. 'They are as I remember them. Or,' she said meditatively, 'even better.'

'It's the water,' said Ernesto. 'They want to change the water. To bring it in, in pipes. But my water comes from Alberto here, and it is special.'

'The snails are special, too,' said Alberto modestly. 'Ernesto gathers them every morning, early.'

'I would like some more, please,' said the Marchesa.

'Well, that was all right!' said the Marchesa, pleased, as they walked away. 'So they still remember me! I told you, didn't I, that they were my people?'

'You did,' said Seymour. 'And that Naples was your place.'

'It is,' said the Marchesa. 'Still.'

'And yet you have also said something different: that Naples was an awful place, the last place you wanted to come to when you were exiled.'

'Be sent to,' corrected the Marchesa. 'By my bastard husband. There is no contradiction. I love Naples and I hate it.'

'Why did your husband send you here?'

'Because,' said the Marchesa, 'he knew that I would hate it.'

'And that you loved it and would find old friends here.'

'You don't know my husband!'

'I'm beginning to. I was wondering if he asked you to look them up. And give them a message.'

The Marchesa looked at him.

'Oh, ho!' she said. 'Is that the way the wind blows?'

She looked at him again. 'No, he didn't give me a message to deliver. And if he had, I wouldn't have delivered it. *Any* message. From him or to them.'

She shook her head.

'All that was a long time ago,' she said. 'That was one of the things I wanted to put behind me. And I had never really had much to do with it. The Hospital kept me away from things like that. And then when I went to Venice I was out of their reach. Of course, when I started singing professionally, I couldn't entirely escape it. Especially when I sang in Naples. But someone like me was always handled with kid gloves, if I was touched at all. I knew about the other side, of course, as everyone who grows up in Naples does. But I wasn't close enough to it to know anyone . . . anyone I might give a message to.'

She shook her head. 'The only thing Alessandro told me when I left was to go and dig a hole in the sea.'

There was a sudden bustle in the *pensione* and baskets appeared full of children's clothes.

'What are we doing to do about all this?' said Giuseppi, gesturing towards the baskets.

'Get Matteo to carry them on his cart,' said Maria.

'Wouldn't that tell people that Jalila is moving?' asked Francesca. 'And then couldn't they find out from Matteo where she had moved to?'

'We could ask Matteo to say nothing,' said Maria, doubtfully.

'Matteo is a blabbermouth,' said Giuseppi.

'I can walk,' said Jalila.

'With all this stuff? And with the children?'

'I must leave the stuff behind,' said Jalila determinedly.

'I will go with you,' said Giuseppi. 'I can carry it.'

'No, you can't,' said Maria. 'And, anyway, wouldn't that give the game away, too?'

'I know!' said Francesca. 'Let's get Giorgio to carry it.'

'Wouldn't that amount to the same thing?'

176

'No,' said Francesca. 'Giorgio is not as close to the family as Grandfather is. And also . . .' She thought. 'Couldn't we pretend it was something to do with the race? Giorgio is working on that already. He could borrow the cart, put Jalila's things in it and then put something to do with the race on top. Some of those water skins, for instance. He could say he was taking them out to places along the route. And he could go separately, not with Jalila, and so no one would connect them.'

Maria looked at Francesca approvingly.

'That's a good idea, Francesca,' she said.

'I'll go and get him,' said Francesca, and ran off.

Jalila sat down on a chair.

'Biscuit!' said the little boy.

'Come with me,' said Maria, taking him by the hand and leading him off into the kitchen.

The little girl came up to Chantale.

'Can I touch your hair, Signora?' she whispered.

Chantale bent her head.

'Why should it be like this?' said Jalila, bewildered. 'What have I done? What has Bruno done?'

Seymour had been asking himself that, too. What had Jalila done that the Camorra should so suddenly have turned against her? Giuseppi and his friends taking their name in vain, the pension, surely all that was nothing to them? The fact that she was an Arab? But that didn't seem to have mattered much in practice in Naples. It hadn't mattered much to Alessandro in bringing her here in the first place –

He stopped.

'Jalila,' he said, 'you sent a letter to someone in Rome. What did you put in it?'

'My thanks,' said Jalila, surprised. 'It was to my patron. My thanks for bringing me here. I had written before, of course, to do that, soon after I arrived. I had used the same letter-writer as I knew he could do it. But this time I was thanking him for the money he had sent me through Signor Scampion. I should have thanked him before. For that and for Signor Scampion's kindness, when

177

he was so unhappy himself. About the war. I told Signor Alessandro that. I said it was the action of a good man who could think of others. And I said how cruel it was that he should have died in the way that he did. God would not let it go unpunished. That was all I wrote, Signor Seymour. That was all.'

Chapter Thirteen

Jalila went off hand in hand with her children.

Giuseppi wanted to go with her but Maria shook her head.

'People are used to seeing her wandering about with the children,' she said. 'If they see you with her they'll wonder why.'

'Just part of the way,' Giuseppi persisted. 'To make sure she gets out of the city safely. The first part is the dangerous part.'

Maria shook her head.

'Not you,' she said. She thought for a moment.

'Bruno?' she said.

Then she shook her head again.

'Not Bruno,' she said. 'They may be watching him. I know they say it's all right between him and them now, and he says it's all right. But I don't trust them. And while it may be all right for him, it's not all right for her. Best leave him out of this.'

Chantale suggested Seymour.

'And I could go with him,' she said. 'People are used to seeing us walking around and they wouldn't think anything of it. And they don't associate us with Jalila.'

That was thought acceptable and, soon after Jalila left, Seymour and Chantale set off after her, keeping a discreet distance behind. They followed her to the edge of the city and watched her start out on the white, dusty road that led through fields and olive trees to the distant hills where the village was. There was nothing in either dress or appearance – she was no browner than the occasional man she passed working among the olive trees – to distinguish her from any other woman going out from the city to visit relatives in the mountains. It came to Seymour that she fitted in. Or would do, if only they would let her.

'I am beginning to think,' said Miss Scampion, 'that perhaps it would be as well if I returned to England.'

'I think you may be right, Miss Scampion,' said Seymour. 'It would be better to have family and friends around you to support you.'

'Here everything I see reminds me of Lionel.'

'It cannot but be painful.'

'I have been staying on,' said Miss Scampion, looking hard at Seymour, 'in the hope that I would see whoever was responsible for his death brought to justice.'

'I think that time may not be long deferred, Miss Scampion.'

'Do you really think that, Mr Seymour?' she said sharply. 'Or are you just telling me that to fob me off?'

'I really think that.'

Miss Scampion sighed.

'If I could be sure,' she said. 'If only I could be sure.'

'I think you can be confident.'

'There is something particular that makes you say that?'

'There is.'

'Will it be soon? But perhaps I shouldn't ask you that.'

'I expect the police will shortly be in a position to charge someone with your brother's murder. Of course, it could be months before he comes to trial.'

'It would be enough,' said Miss Scampion, 'to know that someone was being charged. I would feel that I had fulfilled my promise. I promised myself, you see, – I promised *Lionel* – that I would not leave Naples until I had seen the man who murdered him being held responsible.'

'I think that time might not be far distant, Miss Scampion.'

'Then I can leave. And perhaps I *should* leave.'

180

'Perhaps you should.'

'I think of Lionel every day,' she said, 'but, you know, I am becoming more and more confused. It was all simple once. We were so contented together. I thought I knew him as well as the palm of my own hand. But lately I have come to feel . . . to feel that I did not know him as well as I thought I did. There were things . . .'

She found it difficult to speak.

'. . . things that I think now he was deliberately keeping from me. That betting slip. That dreadful woman, the Marchesa. I knew about her, of course, but I did not suspect that their relationship was . . . as I think now that it was. And then . . . then that other woman. Not an Englishwoman. Not even . . . not even . . . an Italian!'

'Miss Scampion –'

She held up her hand. 'I know what you are going to say, Mr Seymour. That I should not jump to conclusions. But how can I not conclude when the evidence was before my eyes? I saw them, Mr Seymour, I saw them! But I refused to believe it. I kept on denying it to myself. But then when he died it was as if his death suddenly unlocked a flood of things that had been there all the time and that I had refused to see, but that all came crashing down on me when we moved to Naples.'

She looked at Seymour. 'And so, Mr Seymour, I shall not be sorry to leave Naples. Especially now after what you have told me. I shall be leaving at the end of the week after completing my arrangements. There are one or two things in the house that I still have to dispose of but that should not take long. Father Pepe is coming over later to take the rest of Lionel's things. And then I shall say my farewells.'

She held out her hand to Seymour. 'Thank you, Mr Seymour, for enabling me to keep my promise. For I am sure you have had a hand in all this.'

She turned to Chantale. 'And thank you, my dear, for your patience with a silly old woman.'

She gave Chantale a quick, unexpected kiss on the cheek. 'I am sure that you will be more successful in managing your life than poor Lionel was. May I wish you

every happiness together? And I hope that your husband
will bring you as much comfort as he has me.'

Bruno was waiting for them in the *pensione* when they
got back.

'It is all right, is it?' he said. 'You saw her go?'

'We watched,' said Seymour, 'and saw her go. And I
don't think anyone else was watching too.'

'God be praised!' said Bruno, sitting down and putting
his head in his hands.

'She will be safe now,' said Maria.

'I hope so, I hope so.'

'You love her, don't you, Bruno?' said Maria gently.

He raised his head. 'Yes. But – but she doesn't love me.'

'It may come, Bruno.'

'No,' he said. 'It won't. It won't. I know that now. I had
hoped . . . But she told me.'

'She may change her mind.'

'She won't.'

He looked at Chantale. 'You were right, Signora. You
tried to tell me but I would not hear. She has a mind of
her own, and it is not my way inclined. She said there was
too much distance between us. And she did not like what
I did – those I worked for. She said it would come to evil.
And she was right.'

'Bruno –' began Maria.

He shook his head. 'There is blood on my hands, Maria.
She didn't know it, but there is.'

'You say these things, Bruno, but –'

'No, Maria. She was right.'

'At least,' said Seymour, 'there is not now going to be
more blood on your hands.'

Bruno gave him a startled look.

'No,' he said quietly.

'Bruno,' said Seymour, 'what was the job they were
going to ask you to do?'

'I – I cannot say.'

'I will say it if you don't.'

182

Bruno looked at him in anguish.

Seymour nodded.

'Go on,' he said.

'To kill Jalila,' Bruno said.

'Bruno!' gasped Maria.

He turned towards her. 'It is true, Maria. But I would never have done it.'

'Of course you wouldn't, Bruno! Of course you wouldn't!'

'Why did they think you would?' asked Seymour.

'Because in Naples you do what they tell you,' said Bruno simply. 'And –'

He stopped.

'There was another reason, wasn't there?'

Bruno shuffled.

'It was a Neapolitan matter, Signor,' he said awkwardly.

'A question of honour?'

'They thought so,' said Bruno bitterly. 'And others thought so. That is important, because if the world thinks so, then your own honour is called in question.'

'And your honour was called into question?'

'Not just my honour,' said Bruno hoarsely.

'Tonio's?'

'Tonio's. And hers.'

'Jalila had done something to bring your honour into question?'

'Yes. I could see that it would,' said Bruno agitatedly, 'and so I spoke to her. I warned her. But she was angry with me and said there was no question of . . . of what I thought, and others were saying.'

'And did you believe her?'

'Yes. *Yes!*' said Bruno passionately. 'My heart spoke, and I believed her.'

'And you were right, Bruno!' said Maria hotly.

'Yes, you were right,' said Seymour.

'But . . .' said Bruno.

'Yes,' said Seymour. 'But . . .'

'I knew she was pure,' said Bruno, 'and couldn't be anything but pure. And true to Tonio. Nevertheless, what

183

had been seen, had been seen, and could not be denied. It couldn't be her fault. So . . .'

'It must be his,' said Seymour.

'Yes. He must have tricked her, taken advantage of her innocence. And ignorance of Naples.'

'It did not happen as you suppose, Bruno,' said Seymour. 'He was innocent, too. He was trying to help her. As someone had asked him to.'

'They were seen –' began Bruno.

'They were both warm people, Bruno. And perhaps they went further than they should. But in their hearts they were as innocent as you know Jalila to be. He was just giving her money. From someone else. As he had been asked to do. That is all it was.'

'Who is this person?' demanded Bruno suspiciously.

'You know him.'

'Why was he giving her money?'

'For the same reason as he had given money before. Through you and Marcello.'

'Alessandro?' said Bruno incredulously.

'Yes.'

'It cannot be!' said Bruno.

'Nevertheless, it was so,' said Seymour. 'Why he sent her money again at that point, I do not know. Perhaps because she had written a letter to thank him, and it had reminded him of her. And he was pretty sure she would be in need. He had no great opinion – unjustly, perhaps, – of your ability to support her. So he sent her money.'

'By the Englishman?'

'Yes.'

Bruno looked stunned.

'Whom you killed, Bruno, believing that he had wronged Jalila.'

'God forgive you, Bruno!' whispered Maria.

'Was it so?' gasped Giuseppi.

'It was so,' said Bruno.

'But . . .' said Seymour.

'But?' said Bruno, turning to him.

184

'That wasn't the only reason why you killed him. Or even the main reason.'

'No,' agreed Bruno.

'You killed him because you had been told to kill him.'

'Yes,' said Bruno. 'That is so. I hesitated when they told me. And they mocked me and said: here is a real virgin! He will not kill even to save his honour, and the honour of his friend! So I killed.'

'You went up behind him,' said Seymour, 'when he was standing at the Porta del Carmine. You knew he often went that way after going out on his bicycle, because you had seen him when you were collecting in the street behind the Porta. Perhaps you had even seen that he sometimes stopped at the Porta. You hid behind the pillar and then stabbed him. And then you ran down the street and hid in a *basso*. Where you were seen, Bruno. As people will tell.'

'This cannot be, Bruno!' said Maria.

'It can, Maria. And it was as he says.'

Seymour took Bruno first to the consulate, where he picked up Richards, and then to the central police station, where he gave Bruno into custody: in Richards's presence, because he wanted an official witness and knew that a consular one would be harder to deny, should the Camorra try to intervene. Although he thought it likely that, for someone as minor as Bruno, they would not even bother.

'But why,' said a still bewildered Richards, as they walked away from the police station, 'did they get involved in the first place?'

'They were asked to,' said Seymour, 'by someone they knew, who had probably done favours for them in the past and was in a position to do more. He himself had come from Naples and was, I think, a pretty tough customer. He might even have worked for them in the past and they could have gone on working together since. I suspect they

185

knew each other pretty well, so when he asked, they had no problem in agreeing.'

'But why did he want them to kill Scampion for him? Scampion! Good heavens, a man less likely to get across someone to that extent, it would be hard to find!'

'He knew something, you see. He had found it out by accident while visiting the army base, and he was about to reveal it to the press. Your informant was quite right. Only what she – and it was a she, wasn't it? The Marchesa? – didn't realize was that it was not the general press he was going to reveal it to but a specialist press, the bicycling press, where, because of the vicissitudes of Italian politics, and, more particularly, bicycling rivalries, Scampion knew it would receive maximum attention.

'He had discovered, you see, that someone was shipping arms out to Libya under the guise of them being bicycle parts. And shipping them to the Libyans, Italy's enemies. You can imagine the furore it would have caused if it had come out. Heads – and the heads of big people – would have rolled. Big business interests, with all sorts of high-level connections with politics, were involved.

'It had to be stopped. And this was the way it was decided to stop it. By arranging for Scampion to be murdered. And once it became clear that he had been transferred to Naples, the way of doing it was obvious.'

'You knew,' said Seymour accusingly: 'so why didn't you stop it?'

'I knew it was *possible*,' said the Marchesa. 'But that was all. When Vincente told me he'd blurted it all out to Alessandro, about the package, I tried to get him to shut up. I told him to forget about it. I mean, what the hell difference would a small quantity of arms make: given that a war was going on. But it was too late. He had already told Alessandro enough to allow him to guess the person he had to thank. And silence.'

The Marchesa shook her head.

'I knew it was possible,' she said, 'but I couldn't believe, somehow, that it *would* happen. That Alessandro would actually do it. I didn't, in fact, think he would until it was too late.'

She was silent for a moment. 'When I heard, well, I was very angry. I tried to think what I could do. It would be no good going to Alessandro and having it out with him. What would that achieve? No one would believe me. The police were in his pocket. All that would come of it would be a blanket indifference and possibly a hole in the sea for me.

'But I had to do something – I felt I *had* to. I couldn't just leave it. Not little Scampion. So I tipped off your Ambassador.'

'But Alessandro, the man who really killed Scampion, will get off scot-free?' said Chantale.

'I am afraid so,' said Seymour. 'I won't be able to pin it on him.'

But someone else had been able to.

Vincente came rushing up.

'Where is Luisa?' he demanded.

'I was talking to her just a few moments ago –'

'Where is she? Does she know? Has anyone told her yet?'

'Told her what?'

'That her husband is dead!'

'Alessandro?'

'He was found yesterday. The news has only just got here. It came to me at the base because – because, well, the army has its own system of communications, you know, and everyone knows about me being Luisa's cousin, and that Luisa was here –'

'Just a minute,' said Seymour. 'Alessandro is dead?'

'Yes!'

'And do you know . . . how he came to die?'

187

'Yes! Oh, it is awful! He was murdered. Stabbed. While he was sitting in his office. They found him lying there. On the carpet!'

'And . . . do they know who did it?'

'A man was seen. Apparently Alessandro knew he was coming. They had instructions to let him in. Otherwise they might not have done. He was a rough-looking man, you see. Of course, Alessandro saw all sorts of people – but he had given instructions and so they let him in. And then the man came out and rushed down the stairs, but they did not go in – they were waiting for Alessandro to tell them, you see – but he didn't, and after a while, a long while, someone – and there he was! Murdered! Oh, what will Luisa think? What will she say?'

What she said was:

'So!' With shock, and then, after a long, hissing intake of breath, again: 'So!'

She shook herself, as a dog shakes itself after going into water.

'So someone caught up with him at last! Well, it was bound to happen sometime. You could not go on as he did. Eventually it would catch up with you. He always said it would. "In Naples," he would say, "you are always only one minute away from the knife."'

She shook herself again. 'But I thought he was . . . charmed. Could get away with anything. That was because he always *did* get away with things. Always! "One of these days you won't," I used to tell him. "Of course, I won't," he said. "It's luck. You have a run with Lady Luck and then the bitch deserts you. She always will desert you in the end. You know that, if you are a Neapolitan. But you can have a good run before the end. You know that, too, if you are a Neapolitan. And so it's worth it."'

The Marchesa gave her shoulders a shake. 'It was a good run with him, the lucky bastard! But in the end his luck ran out. As it always does.'

She turned away.

'I hated him,' she said, over her shoulder. 'And loved him. And he hated me, and loved me. I suppose. And now he's gone! In a typical way, a cheating way. When no one was expecting it. I always thought the police would catch up with him first. But there was no chance of that. He'd got *them* worked out. Coming from Naples, he would have. So there was never any chance of that, really.'

She stopped. 'Unless, of course, they came from outside and he'd not had time to bribe them.'

She looked at Seymour.

'Are you anything to do with this?' she demanded.

'I hope not,' said Seymour. 'But I think I know who is.'

'Yes,' said Bruno. 'I did it. When I went up to Rome. I went to him in his office, I thought he might not see me so I sent in a message. "I am the one who dealt with the Englishman." That was the message and it was enough. He had told them to let me in.

'"What is your name?" he said. "Bruno," I said. "I remember now," he said, "you are a friend of Marcello's." "And Tonio, too," I said. "You asked for my help," he said, "and I gave it. Why do you come to me now?" "Because there is some mistake," I said. "You helped me with Jalila before; and now it is said that you have ordered her to be killed." "Things have changed," he said, "since I agreed to help her." "She is still Tonio's widow," I said.

'He sat there for a moment playing with a pencil. Then he said: "Who sent you?" "No one sent me," I said. "I came to you man to man to put this right." "You do not come from friends in Naples, then?" "No," I said. "They don't know." "Bruno," he said, "in my day Neapolitans were not fools. How has it come about that things have changed?"

'I did not know what to say. He looked at me curiously. "Is it true," he said, "that you are the one who saw to the Englishman?" "Yes," I said. "Well, perhaps you are not quite as stupid as I imagined," he said.

'He thought. And then sighed.

189

'"Or perhaps you are," he said. "Bruno," he said, "did you think this up between you? Or did she think it up for herself?"

'"I don't know what you mean," I said.

'"You didn't decide between you to put the squeeze on me? No, I see you didn't. Then she thought it up all by herself."

'"She didn't think anything up by herself," I said. "She's not like that."

'"But she did, Bruno," he said. "She wrote to me."

'"I don't know anything about that," I said.

'"No, I'm sure that you don't," he said. "You're a good boy, Bruno. Now go home and forget all about her."

'"She's Tonio's widow!" I said.

'He sighed. "For Christ's sake," he said. "Don't you understand? She knows something that I don't want people to know. That Englishman told her. That was why he had to be removed, so that he couldn't tell people. That was why my friends had to call on you in the first place, Bruno. I had hoped that would be an end of it. But then I got this letter. She said that she had been talking to him. That was all right. I had told him to, I had told him to give her some money from me. Well, that was a mistake, and not like me. But I thought, well, maybe she needed it, and for Tonio's sake . . .

'"But, you see, she said she had been talking to the Englishman. And that set alarm bells ringing. What did they talk about? Marcello had told me she was a good girl and a true wife – hell, you had told me that, too – so I knew it couldn't be what you might think. And then something she said in the letter – that something was on his mind. Hell, I knew what was on his mind. It was on my mind, too, and I knew I had to do something about it. I had to stop it getting around. And what she was telling me was that it *had* got around, that she knew about it. She didn't actually say it but what she meant was obvious: it *would* get around unless I coughed up."

'"She's not like that," I said. "She's an innocent."

190

'"Well, you may be right," he said. "Or you may not be right. But I can't risk it. Because if I'm right and you're not right, I could be in big trouble. And not just me, other people. Important people, Bruno. So I can't take the risk. It's got to stop here. There's got to be an end to it. That's why I had to ask them to do it. To take care of her. As they did of the Englishman."

'"They asked me to do it," I said.

'"Jesus!" he said. "They shouldn't have done that! She being Tonio's widow and you being Tonio's friend! It was a mistake."

'"It was," I said. "Because there are other ways of putting an end to it." And I stabbed him.'

Maria crossed herself when Seymour told her.

'Poor Bruno!' she said.

'Poor Bruno!' echoed Father Pepe. He had called in after collecting a bundle of Scampion's things from Miss Scampion and they were sitting around a table having a drink, which Giuseppi said he needed after all this.

'These Neapolitans!' he said, shaking his head. 'They're worse than Arabs.'

'I am a Neapolitan!' said Maria warningly.

'And so am I!' said Francesca.

'No, you're not!' said Giuseppi. 'Only three quarters of you are Neapolitan. The other quarter, which comes from me, is Roman. And it's the only sensible quarter.'

'I am all Neapolitan,' said Giorgio, 'and I will make up for that quarter.'

'Not in brains, you won't!' said Giuseppi.

'How is Jalila?' asked Father Pepe.

'She has gone over to your old village, Father,' said Maria. 'She should be safe there.'

'As long as no one gets to hear,' said Giuseppi.

Giorgio suddenly looked worried.

'Giorgio!' demanded Francesca. 'You have not told anyone, have you? He took Jalila's things over for her,' she explained to Father Pepe.

'I – I may have mentioned –'

'Giorgio! How could you! I told you, I *told* you, not to say anything to *anyone*.'

'It was just a casual remark. Giovanni saw me coming back with the cart and asked me where I had been.'

'And you told him!' said Maria, jumping up from the table. 'You fool!'

'Giovanni is the biggest blabbermouth in Naples!' said Giuseppi, aghast.

'And his cousin is one of Their collectors!' said Maria.

'I am sorry –' said Giorgio.

'Someone must get over there and warn her!' said Maria.

'I will go!' said Giorgio.

'Take your bicycle!' instructed Francesca.

'I – I can't. It's all in pieces. I was working on it. But I will run all the way!'

'Run, then!' said Maria.

Giorgio set off at the double.

'And I will speak to Giovanni,' said Maria.

She hurried out.

'It is not enough just to warn her,' said Francesca. 'She must be moved.'

'I have friends at Ferrara,' said Father Pepe.

Maria came back, her face grim.

'It is too late,' she said. 'He has already told them.'

Father Pepe sprang up.

'I have my bicycle,' he said. 'No one will get there before me.'

He ran out, and a moment later came speeding past the front door of the *pensione* pedalling furiously.

Chapter Fourteen

Seymour, who was a habitual early riser, was up first. Chantale, who was not, was still in bed. Francesca, who normally took after Chantale and had to be roused every morning by Maria to do her chores, had departed from her usual practice and was standing bleary-eyed by the open front door when Seymour came down. She was waiting for Giorgio, who had still not returned.

Maria, up early as was her custom, took in the situation at a glance and at once got Francesca busy; thoughtfully taking care, however, to see that her duties mostly occurred in the dining room, from where she could keep an eye on the door.

Giuseppi, who these days found the night rather long and usually only slept for part of it, appeared early, too. He took in Francesca at the door and then went away again; returning shortly after, however, with his gun. Maria, though, told him to take it away again, and, when he demurred, hissed that if They saw it, it would give the game away.

A crestfallen Giorgio appeared soon afterwards.

Francesca ran to meet him.

'It's all right,' said Giorgio, pushing her off.

He went up to Maria and, to her surprise, kissed her.

'That is from Jalila,' he said gruffly.

'And this one is from Father Pepe,' he added, kissing her again.

'He got there in time?' said Maria, softened.

'Went past me like a rocket,' said Giorgio. 'I don't know

how he does it on that old contraption of his.' He looked at Francesca. 'You know,' he said, 'it's not right that someone like Father Pepe should have to rely on something like that. Oh, it was very good once, I'll give him that. A *very* good machine at the time. Best model available. But it's taken a pounding on those country roads and I think he deserves something better. I was wondering, Francesca – I've got a little money put by and – would you mind, Francesca? It was meant for you.'

Francesca kissed him.

'I think it is a very good idea,' she said. 'You always have such good ideas, Giorgio.'

'Hold on a minute –' began Giuseppi.

'No, I don't,' said Giorgio. 'Mostly I have crap ideas. I should listen to Francesca.'

'Now you're talking!' said Giuseppi. 'You know, Maria, this boy is improving all the time!' He turned to Giorgio. 'And it's all right?' he said. 'Pepe got there in time?'

'They were slow,' said Giorgio. 'They got there just after me, and by that time Father Pepe had sorted it all out. He wouldn't tell me where she's gone, but she's gone.'

Maria crossed herself. 'God be thanked!'

Francesca, unusually, crossed herself, too.

Maria looked at Giuseppi.

'Well, this once,' said Giuseppi, and followed suit.

'He's going to come into Naples tomorrow,' Giorgio said, 'to see the race. And then he'll call on you.'

'Ah, yes,' said Giuseppi, 'the race.'

The big race between the Yellows and the Reds, or, as Naples mostly saw it, between the army and the socialists, was to take place the next day.

Giuseppi was sunk in gloom. He could see no way in which the Reds could avoid a shattering defeat and the Red cause a heavy symbolic blow.

'There's a lot of money on it,' said Giorgio, 'a *lot* of money. And it's all on the Yellows.' He lowered his voice. 'They say Our Friends have come in heavily.'

'And on the wrong side, too, I'll bet,' said Giuseppi, depressed.

'Their money is on the Yellows,' said Giorgio.

'Why?' said Giuseppi indignantly. 'Why does it have to be on the Yellows? You'd have thought they'd have supported the poor!'

'That will be the day!' said Maria.

'Not the army, at any rate,' said Giuseppi. 'What has the Camorra got to do with the army?'

'Too much,' said Giorgio. 'You know, they say there was some sort of racket they were involved in, sending arms out to Libya or something. To Libya! To our enemies!'

'The bastards!' said Giuseppi. 'To make money out of selling arms to Italy's enemies which they can use against our men!'

'It's all wrong!' said Giorgio. 'But there you are, Giuseppi. The Camorra are like the rest of us. If they see a chance to make money, they will!'

'There's a lot of money on the Yellows, is there?' said Francesca thoughtfully.

'Huge. And most of it is Camorra money.'

'What are the odds?'

'A hundred to one on the Yellows,' said Giorgio.

'The shame of it, the shame of it!' groaned Giuseppi, putting his head in his hands.

'Giorgio, you know that money you were going to buy Father Pepe a bicycle with? Can I have it back? Temporarily.'

'Francesca! You are not –' began Maria.

'And you, Grandfather,' said Francesca, turning to Giuseppi, 'you've got some money put by, haven't you?'

'Yes, and I'm not throwing it away on –'

'Not backing the Reds? After all you've said? Oh, the shame of it, the shame of it!!' said Francesca, striking her brow.

'Well, perhaps –'

'And I think Rinaldo will lend me some, and Pietro. And perhaps Lucio. And maybe also –'

195

'Francesca, you realize that if you borrow it, you will have to pay it back?'

'Ah, but with those odds –'

'Francesca, you are not to do this!'

'Haven't you forgotten something?' asked Giorgio. 'For you to skin the Camorra, the Reds have got to win!'

'Well, you're the man with ideas, Giorgio,' said Francesca demurely.

On bicycles Seymour had absolutely no ideas at all. He remembered, however, that Scampion had made notes on possible routes and went round to the consulate to borrow them from Richards.

'It's no use, old man,' said Richards. 'The Yellows have got it sewn up.'

'Everyone thinks that,' said Seymour. 'That's why the odds are a hundred to one.'

Richards whistled. 'A hundred to one! Almost worth taking a plunge at that sort of price. However –'

'Father Pepe is backing the Reds,' said Seymour.

'He is, is he?'

Richards looked thoughtful.

'Look, old chap . . .' he said, after a moment.

Giorgio pored over Scampion's notes with Giuseppi and Seymour.

'If it's going to be anywhere, it's got to be at Paisi,' Seymour said. 'Where, according to Scampion, the road suddenly narrows. "We don't want too many people going into that bit together." That's what he says.'

'I don't see how that helps us,' said Giuseppi. 'We could block it up, I suppose.'

'And then there would be the most God-almighty pileup!' said Giorgio, eyes gleaming.

'The trouble is, it would affect both sides,' said Seymour.

'And if it was too big a pile-up, the race would be

196

declared void,' said Francesca. 'And then we wouldn't get their money.'

'Better to go down fighting,' said Giuseppi fiercely, 'than let the Yellows win!'

'Of course,' said Francesca, 'if we could somehow get the Yellows to let the Reds go in first . . .'

'My heart has always been with the poor,' said the Marchesa.

'They would be a long way in front by then,' said Seymour. 'So far in front that they would think they could afford to stop.'

'Have you got any colours?' asked Chantale.

'I will have,' said the Marchesa, 'by tomorrow.'

'We're banking on them being confident,' said Seymour.

'Ah, they'll be confident, all right!' said Giuseppi.

'Over-confident,' said the Marchesa, 'if I know Italian soldiers.'

'And they will like a bit of swagger,' said Seymour.

'Vincente will certainly like a bit of swagger,' said the Marchesa.

'As they're coming up to the finishing line.'

'People cheering and waving flags,' said the Marchesa, entering excitedly into the spirit of things. 'Girls throwing flowers. Vincente will certainly like that bit. You know, I've had an idea. Why don't we line that narrow part of the road with pretty girls and tell them to throw their arms around the riders' necks? And pull them off?'

'I think we'd better stick to the original plan,' said Seymour.

The day of the race dawned bright. Well, that was not surprising since almost every day dawned bright in Naples. But to Francesca that day dawned particularly bright. The street leading up to the Palazzo was positively bursting with flowers. They clung to the balconies and hung from the window boxes. They garlanded every lamp post and

197

every tree. There were flowers in the windows of the shops and in the hair of the girls.

Francesca herself wore a huge red poppy, presented to her by Giorgio and obtained by stealth from the garden of one of the big hotels. She stood at the scheduled finishing line, along with Seymour, Chantale and Maria, and jumped up and down with excitement.

She could hardly wait for the first riders to appear.

In their Red shirts, she hoped, although now that the moment was at hand she could not still forebodings. Could those dunderheads win even if Giorgio and the Marchesa had set it up for them? Her heart remained obstinately in her mouth.

One thing at least she was to be spared. The Reds would be riding in red but not in sacks. Faced with the prospect of their men revealing themselves to the world in attire which would bring shame to their womenfolk, the riders' wives had rebelled, and had stitched up, according to Maria, something that was quite respectable. Francesca loved her grandmother but had no confidence whatsoever in her fashion sense. She feared the worst, and her confidence was only partly restored by Giuseppi, who had also seen the new kit, denouncing it as a prime example of capitalist decadence.

Red, though, of some kind, it had to be, had to be. Although in her heart she still clung to the svelte lines and subtle tints of the Yellow and Green kit, on this occasion she firmly put aside aesthetic considerations in favour of economic ones. The Yellows, by hook or by crook – and it looked as if it was going to have to be by crook – *had* to lose.

Nevertheless, as she suddenly became conscious of a distant roar at the end of the street, her heart rose sickeningly into her mouth.

Father Pepe was standing nearby and for once Francesca felt a need to have recourse to the Church.

'Will they do it, Father?' she whispered urgently.

'Sure thing!' said Pepe confidently. And then, unfortunately, less confidently: 'I hope.'

But now, yes, yes, they were coming into sight. And tears were blocking her eyes and this dammed gigantic Englishman was blocking her view!

And then Father Pepe was dancing with Maria, and Maria was shouting – surely this could not be so? She would have to check later – 'We've done the bastards!'

And then Francesca couldn't see anything at all because there was a sudden flood of tears in her eyes, but somehow she knew that it was the Reds who were riding triumphantly up to the finishing line.

'Luisa,' said Vincente accusingly. 'It was your fault!'

'My fault?' said the Marchesa, wide-eyed. 'I was only doing what my people wanted!'

It was only afterwards that Vincente, brooding over the events of the day, thought to ask himself exactly what she had meant.

As the Yellows had swept into view – and it was the Yellows, unfortunately there wasn't a Red in sight – Giorgio had run forward waving a huge flag. 'Yellows pull off next left!' Giuseppi, standing in the middle of the road – prepared as ever to sacrifice himself for the revolutionary cause – had ushered them into the lay-by where the Marchesa, unoverlookable in a bright peacock dress and with bright peacock feathers spreading all over the place, not to mention a startlingly-plunging neckline, waited with a huge banner on which were the words: 'Victory and Honour!'

'Victory' alone would probably have done for the army riders but 'Honour' as well was simply irresistible. The Marchesa had greeted them with an inspiring, but rather prolonged, address, given the banner into the hands of what looked to be the fastest riders, and sent them at last on their way.

Too late.

* * *

Francesca had made so much money that she was able to pay off all her creditors and give them a return that left them delirious with joy, set up Jalila in a house of her own in Bologna, buy Father Pepe a splendid new bicycle, and ensure that Giuseppi and Maria need never again be bothered by the prospect of a collector. The Camorra, indeed, had taken such a heavy hit that they had to curtail their activities for some time to come.

Maria, however, was not quite happy. She was glad of the money but knew that it had not been made by working, and she feared that Francesca might be lured into deeper and sinful ways and make a lot more. She consulted Father Pepe, who sighed and said that winning had not helped him much. He suggested that Francesca go to his old university and do a degree in economics or mathematics.

'Although,' he added, 'it may be that they haven't much to teach her. It is a pity that Alessandro is no longer with us, for I am sure he would have found a use for her in his business.'

This was reported to the Marchesa, who had inherited most of Alessandro's wealth, as well, of course, as having plenty of her own. This would need careful handling and she filed Francesca's name for future reference.

She, herself, would enter a convent. When she learned, however, that this could mean her surrendering much of her property, she thought again and decided that she would not actually enter the convent but would support it from outside and visit it from time to time, fitting in her visits to coincide with her duties at the Foundling Hospital, where she was going to help with the singing.

Maria thought this could only do good; to her as well as the children.

The best place from which to view the bay, said Miss Scampion, was from the top of the Vomero hill. There were two ways to go up it; one was by the wire-rope railway, which led up from somewhere at the back of the city, the other was to use the steam lift. This went straight up from the middle of the tunnel which cut through the hill between the city and Pozzudi.

The steam lift, said Miss Scampion, was too small to take bicycles so she preferred the wire-rope railway, which, anyway, gave better views. Seymour and Chantale, on their last evening, decided, however, to come back by that route, so as to take advantage of the glorious, lingering Neapolitan sunset, and go up by the steam lift.

They came out close to a giant pine tree which offered a frame to the lovely panorama of Sorrento and Capri, and also to Vesuvius, wreathed now in the sunset in roseate steam.

When they walked a few yards in the other direction they could see over into the other bay, where the trawlers were putting out to do the night's fishing, and where the small boats of the hand-line fishermen were just flocking back to shore. In the fading light the black sand of Coroglio beach glittered with the silver of newly landed mullet and anchovies.

Seymour wondered if the Marchesa was down there on the quayside with her people, waiting, in the Neapolitan way, for her boat to come in.

Giorgio had been a problem. Ever since her financial coup, he had refused to speak to Francesca. Instead, he talked to Seymour, feeling, he said, the need for a man's point of view.

'How can I marry her?' he asked. 'I couldn't be supporting her: she would be supporting me.'

And that, his Neapolitan sense of male pride would not allow.

Francesca assured him that she didn't actually have any money. She had put it all in trust. Giorgio wasn't quite sure what this meant but felt dubious about it. It sounded like some more of her financial hanky-panky. He consulted Seymour on the point.

Seymour said that it certainly set the money at arm's length but what it meant was that the money would still be there should they ever need it. If, for example, Giorgio's new bicycle shop failed.

'No chance,' said Giorgio confidently. 'The bicycle is the way of the future.'

Or when, said Seymour, there were lots of *bambini* in the house. 'Children eat money,' he said.

'Ah, yes,' said Giorgio, he could quite see that. His brow cleared. Less, however, because he was persuaded by Seymour's argument than because he reckoned that when there were lots of *bambini* in the house, Francesca would have her hands too full to be able to go in for any financial cabbalism.

'And after all,' he said to Seymour, 'a man is a man and a woman is a woman. When we are married she will do as I say.'

'Giorgio –' began Seymour, and then stopped. Who was he to shatter Giorgio's illusions?